D1479255

SOMEBODY'S
WATCHING YOU

SOMEBODY'S WATCHING YOU

Robin D'Amato

atmosphere press

1

Eons ago, as the planet was starting to thaw, a glacier slid down North America, tore an extended strip of land off of what is now the state of Connecticut, and deposited it into the ocean. People built roads on it. They built houses on it. They went to beaches, ate seafood, and eventually, they called it Long Island. I imagined that the further east you traveled on the Island, the richer the houses would get, the nicer the beaches, the posher the people. We were not from that part of the Island. We were about as west as you could get without living in Queens, less than an hour from Manhattan by train, or at four in the morning by car. That other end, we never saw.

I always thought one day I'd leave that belt of glacial refuse. Even as a kid, I had the feeling that I was meant to be elsewhere, and the older I got, the more restless I became. Right on the southwest doorstep of Long Island was the amazing and powerful New York City. I didn't have to go far to experience whole different ways of approaching life. Let the spectators have their tailgating and their 2.2 children and their early retirement plans. My artistic temperament wanted me to create, and I was just sure that, someday, I'd find something wonderful to do in that shiny, distracting, intriguing nugget that was the City.

But then I met Jeff.

My friends and I used to frequent a place in Elmont called Davy's, a comfortable dive that served bar food and hired local bands to play on Friday and Saturday nights. A cover band was playing that night, and they were proficient enough that people began to gather on the open floor space in front of the stage to dance. I was twisting and jumping around, completely immersed in the music, and soon oblivious to the clinking glasses, the smoke wafting into the bar from the smokers outside, the women I knew who were flirting loudly with the bartender, the house music lying in wait to come back on when the band finished its set, or, even, the tallish man with chin-length, caramel-brown hair who was watching me. When the band took a break, he came out of the shadows and approached me.

"You've got some great moves there," he said.

An obvious pick-up line, but I was okay with that. "Thank you."

His looks crept up on me. Not a pretty face, much more rugged, and, at first glance, seemingly average. Then *pow*! The second glance.

"Are you here with anyone?" he said. His eyes crinkled as he smiled, which was not keeping them from piercing through me.

"Just my friends."

"They're anyone," he said. "Can I join you a moment?"

"Sure."

He sat down next to me, and I noticed the athletic build under his long-sleeved t-shirt.

"I'm Jeff."

"Melody."

"So, what do you do, Melody?"

"I freelance. Interior design. You?"

"I'm a fill-in DJ at a small station here on the Island. I've been looking for a full-time gig, so, fingers crossed."

His smile was killing me. I played with my mousy-brown hair and tried not to stutter. "You do have a good DJ voice," I said.

"I do? Why do you say that?"

"It's distinctive. You have that deep, friendly, 'I'm on the air' tone."

"Well, they did teach me 'radio voice' in broadcasting school. Do I have an AM voice or an FM voice?"

"I think it can go either way."

My friends returned to the table with their next round of drinks. They both raised their flawlessly groomed eyebrows.

"Melody. Who's your friend?"

"This is Jeff," I said. "Jeff, Carrie and Ann."

"Sorry, ladies. Didn't mean to invade your table."

He started to stand up, but Carrie, who was tall and stocky with an equally large personality, put her hand on his shoulder and said, "Sit. You can invade our table any time."

The neon signs behind the bar were making his green eyes twinkle, and I felt an overwhelming urge to tell my friends to back off. I wasn't so worried about Ann. She understood the right of possession. Carrie, however, was working on her fourth beer. She sat on the other side of him and pushed her seat against his.

"Can we buy you a drink?"

"No, thank you. I'm driving."

I was drinking seltzer, myself, since I was the designated driver of our trio. No one would want the other two, especially Carrie, behind a wheel in their respective conditions.

The band came back to the stage, which was a platform that just about accommodated the four musicians. Jeff kept turning his head to smile at me, even though Carrie had wrapped herself around him like a squid, holding him so close that her platinum-blonde, permed hair was draping over his shoulder. He moved his chair closer to mine and turned it to face the band. We had to yell to hear each other.

"You know, these guys have a bit of a McGuiness Flint thing going on with that mandolin," Jeff said.

I couldn't believe he mentioned that band. "McGuiness Flint? 'When I'm Dead and Gone,' McGuiness Flint?"

"You've heard of them? They're a 70s band."

"I love that song. My mother had the single. Used to play it for my brother and me when we were kids."

"No kidding. I picked up their LP at Cutler's Records a few years ago. Thought it was cool they had a mandolin player."

"What's a mandolin?" Carrie asked. I thought she probably knew; she was just trying to be part of the conversation.

Jeff leaned over the table and pointed. "That instrument over there."

Carrie shifted her chair closer to him. Ann, who was pretending to ignore her and watch the band, threw me a sympathetic side glance.

Each cover the band played, Jeff would turn to me and say who did the original and what year. After a few songs, I told him an original band and the year.

"You know your music," he said with a smile.

"Big fan of WCBS, when it was an oldies station. I used to listen to it in high school." I realized I had just revealed my age to this music encyclopedia. Not that thirty-something was that old.

"I liked WNEW," he said. "Always wished I could have worked there. But they were gone by the time I got out of broadcasting school."

Fueled by music and alcohol, the dancers in front of the band were gyrating more freely and began bumping into the tables nearest the stage. The musicians eventually took a short break so their front man could introduce the other players. Jeff pushed his chair back and stood up.

"You're not going," Carrie said.

"Got to. Got the early shift tomorrow."

Carrie got up and put her hand on his arm, but before she could say anything, he said, "Anyway, nice to sit with you gals. I really just wanted to come over here to give Melody my number and get hers, if she'll give it to me."

He reached into his wallet and handed me his card.

"Yes, of course." I gave him my business card.

"Call you soon," he said.

He wasn't gone two minutes when my phone rang.

"Told you I'd call soon."

I laughed. "Are you even out of the bar?"

"Nope. Just by the exit. Anyway, we'll talk soon."

"Does that mean you're going to call me from the corner?"

He laughed. "Do you want me to?"

He used to have a big, hearty laugh. That was more than ten years ago. These days, he hasn't been laughing at all. It has been months.

I climbed the stairs to our bedroom, sat on the edge of the bed, and put my hand on Jeff's shoulder. The curtains were still drawn, letting in just a tiny ray of sunlight. Jeff turned towards me. His green eyes were grey, a color they turned when he was sick or depressed. He tried to smile, but then turned back. It didn't look like up was happening today. I sat there a little while longer, then went down to the kitchen.

I washed my dishes from breakfast. The window over the sink had a view of our bird feeder. Poor things; half the time, I would forget to fill it. There was one forlorn chickadee perched on the feeder, and feeling guilty, I went outside and filled it. There. I accomplished something. Back inside, I watched the birds crowd around. How did they know there was suddenly food there?

I heard the shower turn on. Jeff had gotten up, although sometimes he would lose his momentum after his shower and end up back in bed. His skin was getting this amazing, soft sheen to it from all of the showers he was taking. There were no dead skin cells anywhere on his body. On days when he was especially motivated, he shaved, too. At least he wasn't turning into a Wookiee.

While I waited to see whether Jeff would be coming

downstairs, I went into our music room and looked over his huge album collection. He had everything from the sublime to the unplayable. Really. Hard core punk? Noise? Tiffany? The eclectic nature of his musical tastes was not, by the way, a symptom of his mental illness, although he did have an inexplicable fascination with Britney Spears. Even before, when things were going well, he'd play the Monkees, then the Buzzcocks, then Killcode, then Benny Goodman. He liked to mix things up.

I carefully surveyed all the different categories then picked my usual: the Beatles. They made me happy. I normally had an elaborate process of selecting music, but these days I kept it simple. I chose a CD and put it in the player. Music was the only thing lately that was keeping me from crawling back into bed with Jeff. The album played long enough for me to be engrossed, and then, in the middle of "I Want You (She's So Heavy)," Jeff appeared in the doorway.

"Melody?"

He was wearing just his robe. Several months earlier, I would have taken that as an invitation to go upstairs with him and, literally, disrobe him. That would not be happening today. Not sure when that might happen again. That robe had been with him since college, and, disheveled as it was, he was reluctant to replace it. It was a great shade of steel blue, and he never saw another color he liked quite as much.

"Hey, Jeff. You hungry? I'll make you something." He was getting so emaciated from not eating, it was alarming. I made scrambled eggs, cheese, and toast. He tore into it. Yeah, he was hungry. He needed to eat, like, ten plates of that.

"Do you mind if I go out for a little while?" I said. "I want to go shopping. Wanna come?"

He swallowed and looked sad. "Not today. I... uh ... just not today."

"That's okay. It's all good."

"But you can go; I'm alright here. I think I'm going to listen to some music."

"Okay. Good."

It had been a couple of days since I'd been out. I headed to a shopping center not far from our house. Being a nervous driver, I drove at exactly the speed limit, maybe a little under. I signaled like a crazy person; I took a long time to turn into traffic, and I slowed down to let people pass me. This did not make me a favorite among Long Island drivers or, truthfully, any other drivers.

It was a Tuesday, late morning, that weird time between breakfast and lunch where I usually found it hard to figure out what to do with myself. I spent some time trying on shoes I couldn't afford and then settled on a pair that I could. I hoped the young man who was helping me didn't work on commission. He was working hard for that one pair of Aerosoles.

I stopped at the market, then went home. Jeff was still listening to music. All things considered, this was a good sign.

When Jeff and I got married, we took up residence in the town of Floral Park. Our house had a huge picture window that had a built-in seat I covered with cushions from West Elm and three rooms that were meant to be bedrooms. I made one into an office, the one with the over-sized, glass-paned pocket door was Jeff's music room, and our actual bedroom was the master upstairs. We got close to our neighbors, Jeanine and Tom Giordani, right away; although, I hadn't seen them for a couple of months now. I'd taken a temporary furlough from work in hopes of helping Jeff through whatever this was, which meant I was home a lot. If you don't leave the house, you don't see many people.

His doctor had prescribed antidepressants when Jeff first got sick, but they were still in their bottle in the medicine cabinet. His mother had suggested I put them in his food, but that was a trust I wasn't willing to destroy. I talked to Jeff's mother a lot lately. Marie, who rose with the chickens and assumed everyone else did too, would call Jeff's phone first thing in the morning, and when he didn't answer, would call me.

"Did he get up today?"

It was Sunday. *I* was barely up.

"Not yet, Marie." I used to call her Mrs. Hollenback, but she didn't like that. "You're Mrs. Hollenback," she had said. "Call me Marie."

"Well, did you try to wake him? Maybe he would want to go to church."

Jeff never went to church, even when he wasn't depressed. I wasn't sure what she was thinking.

"I'll try to wake him in a little bit. It's still early for us."

"Well, he's got to eat. Will you bring him something?"

I understood. Neither of us had any control over this. We wanted to do something, but there was nothing we could do. On the other hand, she was starting to annoy me.

"I'll try, but I can't force feed him."

There was silence on the other side of the line.

"Well..." She trailed off.

I found my compassion. "I know. This is awful. None of us can do anything."

Marie and I had been bonding these past several months over our common frustrations and heartache. Jeff's father, Frank, didn't want to talk about it, and Jeff had no siblings. Marie was dealing with this alone. As for me, my parents were long gone, and I had a brother I wasn't close to. I used to work, so I had that, and I had gotten myself a therapist, but most days, I, too, handled Jeff on my own. It made sense that we'd be commiserating.

Jeff came downstairs sometime later, and we had lunch together. I was worried he'd go back to bed after we ate, but he surprised me and turned on the television. I curled up next to him and we watched the Three Stooges marathon. Jeff didn't even like the Stooges. Neither did I. We were clearly desperate people.

After three more days of down, Jeff got out of bed. In the meantime, I had cleaned the house, cooked a lasagna, baked a couple of pies, organized the closets, and was contemplating painting the back porch. He woke early, took a shower, shaved, and joined me for breakfast. Halfway through our pancakes, he said, "You know, I think I'll take the car out today."

This was not completely unheard of. He liked to go for a drive once in a while, usually just around town and back, maybe get a haircut. I tried to play it cool.

"Do you have an errand to run?"

"No. I just thought I'd take a drive."

"Uh... Should I come with you?"

He looked sad. "Is it okay if I go alone?"

"Of course."

He actually smiled. Not a big one, but it was there.

"You're the best," he said. He finished eating then went upstairs to put on some clothes. I wasn't sure how long this up time would last. Would he take the car and then need to be rescued?

Just before he left, he stopped at the door, and turned to me.

"You know, Melody...." He paused longer than was natural, and I waited for him to complete his sentence. "The Devil always wins." Then, seeing the look on my face, he added, "It's just an observation. He doesn't have to play by the rules, and we do. That's why the human race will never get ahead of him."

I had no idea how to react to this. He continued.

"But we just have to keep fighting him. That's how it works. That's our job."

He kissed me and headed to the car.

Okay, what brought that on? I rejected the urge to fling myself to the ground, grab his ankles, and beg him not to leave. I couldn't follow him everywhere and protect him from himself, could I? That was what my therapist said, anyway. Despite taking a few moments to talk myself out of it, I followed him out the door. He was already backing up the car, and I was frantic.

Since Jeff became depressed, I had been trying to have

a *Be-Here-Now* kind of attitude. I even bought a necklace with a yin-yang symbol on it, to remind me to chill the hell out. Right now, I was trying to think practically. With Jeff out of the house, I could strip the bed and collect the laundry. I used to be a functioning woman in society with an interesting job that paid well. Now, I spent a lot of my time doing household chores. I never pictured myself as a housewife. Back when things were normal, we both had jobs, and we could afford someone to do the cleaning.

We could also afford two cars.

I soon found that my Zen attitude was failing me. I was worried about what Jeff had said. It wasn't normal. It wasn't even Jeff-is-depressed normal. The thing was, I believed Jeff was wrong. No side wins. In the yin-yang symbol, one side isn't bigger than the other. But I was concerned: why had he come up with this now?

I dropped the laundry and the bedding where I stood and picked up my phone. My therapist had said I could call her anytime if I had an emergency. Jeff talking about the Devil seemed like an emergency.

I guessed she wasn't in session with somebody, because she picked up.

"Melody. What's wrong?"

"Hi, Dr. Osgood. Jeff said the strangest thing this morning and then left in the car. I don't know what to do."

"Do you think he plans to hurt himself?"

Why do you think I'm calling you?

"I don't know. I didn't, but then—"

"We've talked about this. You can't save him from himself. There's nothing you can do."

"But he said—"

"Let's talk about you."

14

Dr. Osgood could be really infuriating sometimes. I didn't want to talk about me. I needed Jeff advice.

"Start with why you think this is an emergency."

Like I said: Infuriating.

"Because he said, 'The Devil always wins.' What the hell is that supposed to mean?"

"Did you ask him?"

"His explanation didn't make sense."

"Then how do you know this is an emergency?"

"Well... I guess I don't."

"I know it's scary. He's not well, and he took the car. There's nothing you could have done to stop him, and there's nothing to do now except wait for him to return."

Okay. In her messed-up way, she talked me off the ledge. Oh, joy. I could go back to doing the laundry.

Long Island was all about the car culture, but I was, at best, ridiculously cautious. My parents were killed in a car accident when I was twenty-two. Some thirty-something jerk sped through a red light and walked away from the accident; my parents did not. Since then, I've driven like a student driver, and I rarely drive alone if I don't know the area.

When our second car was too old to be driven anymore, we decided we'd live with just one car. By that time, only I was working, and interviews for Jeff were scarce. Our lives became smaller. Jeff joined a gym within walking distance from the house. When we could, we made back-to-back doctor and dentist appointments. If one of us had the car, the other was on his own.

Jeff was gone for hours. Without a car, I couldn't really go anywhere, so I did two loads of laundry, folded it, and put it away. I told myself I could always call him if I was that worried. I hadn't gotten any calls from hospitals or the police, so I assumed he was still alive and responsive. I prepared a dinner, which he might or might not eat, that I could pop in the oven when he returned.

If he returned.

I clutched my yin-yang charm. Melody, positive thoughts. He would return, he was fine. Deep breaths. Deep breaths.

My phone rang.

Oh, no…

It was Jeff's mother. Not the police. Not the hospital. Not the morgue.

"How's my boy doing?"

"Well, he got up today. In fact, he took a drive."

"A drive. Oh, dear…"

No kidding.

"He seemed okay when he left, so we'll see." Yes, I lied. I didn't know how to explain what he said to me, so I left it out.

"Has he eaten?"

"Actually, yes."

"Okay. That's good." She paused. "How are you doing?"

I was an emotional wreck, but I didn't want to add to her stress by telling her that.

"I'm coping. Taking each day as it comes."

"He's lucky he has you."

"Thank you."

This wasn't how she used to feel. She changed her tune

since Jeff became ill. I heard the car pulling into the driveway as I was hanging up, and I went to the door. Jeff had gotten his hair cut, it was unusually short, and he was smiling broadly, an unnatural smile that didn't really go with his face. What was that about? And what was he carrying?

"Hey, Melody." Like it was the most normal thing in the world. "I bought Chinese food."

There went my dinner. It would keep. I'd freeze it.

"Uh... great." I had to ask, "You look so happy. What's going on?"

It was highly possible that he was experiencing some form of manic episode.

"I met someone," he said, and headed to the kitchen.

What?

"Uh, Jeff...." I followed him. Clearly, I didn't hear him right. "Did you just say, you met someone?"

He held up a book he was carrying. It was by E. W. Peabody.

I was confused. "Isn't he dead?"

Jeff's bizarre smile was starting to unnerve me.

"Well. Yes. I didn't meet *him*. I met Floyd."

"Floyd?"

"Yes. Floyd. Nice guy. We talked for hours, me and Floyd and his friends from the center. They said I'd really dig this book."

E. W. Peabody was the founder of the Church of Philomathics, so I assumed that that was the center he was referring to. The Church was well known for having quite a few celebrity members, and there was some tax-exemption controversy a while back, but I didn't know much about it other than that. I'd seen endless television commercials for books by Mr. Peabody, books I thought were some kind of self-help volumes, kind of like Tony Robbins. They had Philomathic centers all over the world, and one was not far from our house. Did something happen there to make Jeff spring to life? Would it keep him out of bed? If so, who was I to argue? I would, however, refuse to wash any magic underwear. Wait. Maybe that was the Mormons.

Jeff started humming a Britney Spears song and continued unpacking the Chinese food. "Chow Fun?"

He was still sporting that disquieting smile. For a moment, I wasn't sure if I preferred him up or down.

2

Let's get one thing straight. I didn't believe in miracles. I didn't think that morning Jeff just woke up and was suddenly well again, though it was kind of nice to have him around the house instead of hiding under the covers. He started getting up before noon, eating more than once a day, sitting with me, talking to me. I liked his hair longer, but it would grow back.

Among other unsettling thoughts, this was one I was having now: Did this mean I would have to read this E. W. Peabody book? I had no interest in joining a cult, which I was starting to believe this was. Trust me; I wasn't good at normal religions. I would really suck at being in a cult. But if this was what he was interested in now, if this was what was literally getting him out of bed, shouldn't I at least read the Table of Contents?

I had been going stir crazy lately staying around the house. A guy who was in bed all of the time didn't need a lot of attention. I was starting to think that maybe I should just go back to work. We had been living on our savings, and I was a little worried my job wouldn't be there by the time Jeff was better. Now that Jeff was behaving less *Walking Dead*, I was wondering what I should be doing with myself. While he was in the music room, listening to the soundtrack from *El Topo* and reading his book, I called work.

"Gemini Designs. This is Laura."

"Hey, Laura."

"Melody? How's everything going?" She put her hand over the receiver and called out, "Everyone! Melody's on the phone!" Then she came back and said, "More importantly, how's Jeff doing?"

"He seems a little better."

"Do you think you might be coming back?"

"Well, I was calling to see what my options might be."

"Really? Great! Let me get Carol."

Carol was our Human Resources person. She was really helpful, if she liked you. Laura put me on hold. For some unfathomable reason, the hold music was Kenny G. The office was a hip interior design studio. They could have chosen better hold music.

Carol picked up. "Hi, Melody. I hear things have improved?"

"Things seem better, yes. I just wanted to get an idea of what I would have to do to come back."

"Well, I'll need to check with Anton on the needs of the department. But if everything is okay, we'll just need to do some paperwork and get you back on the payroll."

Considering they had promised me that I could come back at any time, Carol's answer was really irritating.

Anton was the Creative Director. He would want me back. I was sure of that. I had been the Art Director, and while I wouldn't be coming back to that specific job right away, I was more experienced than the other designers who worked there, and he counted on me. Of course, what was true six months ago may not still be true. I shook that idea out of my head. Positive thoughts. Positive thoughts.

Jeff was calling for me. I headed into the music room. He was taking a CD out of the player and putting on an LP.

"Thought you'd want to sit with me."

He smiled at me, that crazy, mysterious smile, and the LP started playing: McGuiness Flint.

I don't know why I didn't tell Jeff that I had called work. Maybe I thought it would jinx him. He did seem better, for sure. Jeff said his new friends didn't approve of antidepressants, though, or any other kind of medicine, except maybe Tylenol, so those meds in the bathroom cabinet remained untouched. Maybe he really didn't need them. He seemed to be on the road to being a functioning human being again.

There was still one thing that was missing: Jeff's sense of humor. He hadn't laughed in months, and although he was now sporting that forced smile, there still wasn't the slightest hint of a laugh coming out of him. That's why I was still worried. Jeff was not Jeff without laughter.

He carried that E. W. Peabody book with him everywhere, so I couldn't even take a peek. I would have thought his friends would want Jeff's wife to join the fold. In fact, I assumed they would have insisted.

While Jeff was reading out in the porch room (this was probably the third reading of that book, by my calculations), I had an idea. I went into my home office and got on the internet, more specifically, Wikipedia. I needed a clear idea of Philomathics:

> "The Church of Philomathics states that a human is a spiritual being (called a *dekan*) that inhabits a physical body. The dekan has had innumerable past lives that, preceding the dekan's arrival on Earth, were spent on other planets."

Lots of people believed in past lives and extra-terrestrials. I wasn't one of them, but at least I got the premise. If this was floating Jeff's canoe these days, I would support him.

"Hi."

Jeff appeared in the doorway. I quickly changed my Wikipedia entry to brussels sprouts. That made as much sense to me as anything else these days. He didn't question it.

We had always said that, one day, we would move to Manhattan. There, they had better restaurants, better pizza, better music, better radio stations, more things to do. Instead, Jeff found a job DJing for an album-oriented-rock (AOR) radio station here on the Island, WXLI. Yes, Jeff used to have a passion. He worked at the station for over a decade, until they switched their format over to sports talk, which Jeff knew nothing about and didn't care to learn. I was thinking his depression might have been a delayed reaction to losing a job he loved and was never able to replace. Many stations in the area, having switched over to preprogrammed music, had stopped hiring on-air personalities. His job prospects had been literally taken over by computers.

Our first date was a tour of record stores. There used to be quite a few of them on the Island, even just a dozen years ago. He bought something in every store and, of course, had to give me the history.

And there were some surprises.

"Neil Diamond?"

"He was a great song writer, especially before he had his nervous breakdown in the late 70s."

"Nervous breakdown?"

"Before 'You Don't Bring Me Flowers.'"

"Oh. That nervous breakdown."

He laughed. "He wrote for Jay and the Americans, Glen Campbell, the Monkees, not to mention his own stuff. He was everywhere."

"And now he's in Vegas."

"At least he's somewhere."

One store we went to had a whole bin of bootlegs. Jeff flipped through them to see if they had anything interesting.

"They must have just gotten someone's collection. These weren't here last month."

He picked something out, then said, "Oh, they also have the Lennon WNEW broadcast."

"What's that?"

"Lennon guest DJ'd on WNEW in 1974. He played songs from his own collection. Good stuff. He even did the commercials. Legendary radio station, legendary musician, on one album."

He added that to his pile.

He found some other bootlegs he liked, some Led Zeppelin, some Who. He also picked up some other non-bootleg stuff, new bands I had never heard of. He flipped through the albums, stopping to read the liner notes or whatever information was on the album covers. I wandered over to the doo-wop section. He quietly approached me and looked over my shoulder.

"You have a turntable?"

"Nope."

He laughed.

"If you like something, I can put it on a CD for you."

"Really?"

He smiled. "Pick something out. Or would you rather I DJ a CD for you of great doo wop?"

"Oh, yes. That."

He made many CDs for me over the years. I had a little stash of them in one corner of the music room. The rest of the room was all Jeff's, although he let me play anything I wanted.

Jeff had gone out earlier to meet up with Floyd and left me alone in the house. I hadn't been in the music room by myself for days. I decided I'd throw on Winona Oak and give the Beatles a rest. I put the CD on the stereo and sat down. To my left, on the seat of the other chair, was a pile of books, their spines facing away from me. I turned them around.

Three books by E. W. Peabody.

This was getting serious.

And weird.

Floyd convinced Jeff that what he needed was three weeks of something called "purging." If Jeff knew what this entailed, he wasn't telling me, just that it required long hours at the center.

"What is this for? What are they purging you from?" I was trying not to sound upset, but I think I was failing.

If Jeff was concerned about my reaction, he didn't let on.

"Marijuana."

"Marijuana? But... you haven't had a joint in months."

The doctor I had brought him to had already suggested stopping marijuana use, that it might help him fight the depression. Jeff had been so down that he had actually lost interest in it long before, anyway.

"Floyd says the toxins might still be there."

I wasn't going to win this fight. I sighed. "Okay. Will they keep you... there, or will you be coming home?"

He smiled that insane smile. "Of course, I'll be coming home."

I looked on Wikipedia to see what they said about purges. Apparently, it entailed "large quantities of vitamins, extensive manual labor, and hours in a sauna." Like Jeff needed to be in some hot, steamy, isolation tank. He was already taking a million showers. His skin was going to peel right off.

Since Jeff had stopped exhibiting his usual signs of depression, I had to figure that whatever the folks at the center were doing for him was worthwhile. He was going to be gone six hours a day, starting the next week, and with his depression seeming to be abating somewhat, I decided I could tell Jeff I was thinking of returning to work.

There was no problem there. He just gave me that goofy smile and said, "I think that's great."

Anton was supposed to call me Friday to discuss my reentry. I was waiting by the phone, then realized, *uh, Melody, it's a cell phone. Put it in your pocket.* I had also decided that, with Jeff coming back to life as he had, I would take up running again. Floyd was supposed to stop by to bring Jeff a new book, so since Jeff would be busy, this was an opportune time for me to leave the house. While he was taking a shower, I got into some sweats and left a note. This was maybe my fourth day out, so I still wasn't covering much territory, and I certainly wasn't clocking my progress. I just jogged around the neighborhood, headed to the park, then sat on my favorite bench, the one nearest the entrance, until I was ready to run again.

We were having a perfect, fall, non-weather day. The trees were happily exuding reds and oranges and yellows. This morning run was taking longer, simply because I fell in love with the foliage. When I got home, Jeff was waiting for me in the doorway. He looked angry.

"Where were you?"

"I left you a note. I was jogging."

"I know, but Floyd was coming over. You missed him," he barked. This was so un-Jeff-like, I was afraid of him. I didn't attempt to enter the house.

"I thought he was coming over to see you," I said. "I didn't think it mattered that I went out."

"Well, it did. And it does. Floyd is a busy man, and he has decided to help me. The least you could do is show some civility and be here to meet him."

Whoa. I'd never seen Jeff like that. What I wanted to

say was, "What the hell is the matter with you?" but I didn't think that would go over very well.

"I'm... sorry," I said, hoping that would calm him down.

He suddenly looked sad. "Well... I'm sorry, too." Then, after we stood there staring stupidly at each other, he said, "Want to come in?"

He stepped aside to let me in, and, with some hesitation, I entered the house. This was when he grabbed me and held me. I wasn't sure whether I should be enjoying this, be afraid, or be worried. I couldn't see his face; I couldn't see anything, because my back was toward him. And I couldn't move, he was holding me so tightly.

It seemed like we stood there for five minutes. Maybe not, but, anyway, much longer than a normal hug should take, even from Jeff. He finally let me go, turned to me, smiled that very weird smile, and said, "Lunch?"

Over the past few weeks, I had concluded that Dr. Osgood was useless. But after Jeff's outburst and that weird hug, I decided I should make an appointment to see her. I might not have been a big fan of hers, but going to see her gave me someone objective to talk to. I spent the hour talking about Jeff, a subject she usually preferred I not talk about ("Let's talk about you," she would say.), but the whole cult and miraculous recovery thing seemed to fascinate her. I'd find it fascinating too, if it weren't directly affecting my life.

I wanted my Jeff back.

I was beginning to learn an important lesson: People

find things out, even if, or especially if, you don't tell them.

Marie called me Monday morning while Jeff was off being "purged."

"So, what's this about Jeff joining Philomathics?"

Did Jeff tell her? I certainly didn't. "I don't know. It baffles me. But it's getting him out of bed."

"Do you know anything about it? All I know is there are celebrities who are avid followers."

"I had a minute to check Wikipedia. Apparently, they believe in past lives and aliens. I didn't get any further than that."

"Well, how does he seem? Does he act like he's in a cult?"

Well, yes. But I said, "Hard to say. He certainly seems to function better than he has been these past several months."

Marie thought this over a minute before she spoke again.

"Well, you'll keep an eye on him, won't you?"

"God, yes."

She sighed. "Okay. I guess we'll have to wait and see."

This would be my first day of work in months. Floyd had picked up Jeff early to go to the center, so this left me alone to decide what to wear. I'd been living in jeans, no makeup, no fanfare. Now I had to be presentable. I chose black pants and a pattern blouse, and I had plenty of shoes to choose from. My hair was naturally wavy, but I put some product in it to keep it neat and a bit shiny. It took me a minute to remember how to apply makeup, but I managed, and I didn't look like a clown.

I was feeling a touch nervous as I pulled into the parking lot. Talking to Carol on the phone had made me insecure, but then Anton greeted me warmly, and I felt normal again. I always thought he was a bit odd looking. He had a horizontally oval face, and his black, curly hair was piled high on top of his head. He wore oversized black-framed glasses, flared pants, usually some kind of linen shirt, and deck shoes. He could pull it off, though. Maybe only I thought it was eccentric.

He set me up to work with Tamara and Laura on their project. Laura, a junior designer, had been with Gemini for only two years. She was maybe five feet tall, and I think her thick brown hair weighed more than she did. She and her husband, Roger, lived in Floral Park, and before I took my temporary leave, we'd sometimes ride home together. Tamara, the lead on this project, used to live in the City, in Chelsea, with her husband, Dave. Dave got relocated to the Island, and Tamara ended up at our design studio. While there was some tension among other senior designers at Gemini, Tamara and I never had that problem. She referred to herself as "the token black," and even though she was clearly being facetious, I had to admit it made me cringe. Tamara was too talented to be the token anything, but it was true that the design team was almost entirely made up of white women. There was one male designer, Rod, who worked with the international group. He was, therefore, "the token male."

When I got home, not only was Jeff there, he was with several people who were strangers to me. There was a tall, ungainly guy standing in front of everyone, who I assumed to be Floyd. He was balding dramatically through the middle of his head, with tuffs of white hair growing on either side, and he was sporting square wire-rim glasses. I don't know if it was because of the glasses, but his eyes had a lifeless, mannequin quality to them. Everyone else in the room was sitting, some on the couch, some on the floor. All conversation stopped abruptly, and they all turned, in unison, to look at me.

"Melody." Jeff wasn't smiling.

I was thinking that I should check the address to make sure this was my house.

"Jeff... Introduce me to your friends?"

I was right about which one was Floyd. The rest of them were so homogeneous I couldn't tell them apart, even the women. They were all staring at me like meerkats sensing danger.

"Well, I'll leave you to your meeting." *Or whatever this is.* I slowly backed out of the room.

I went upstairs. There were more E. W. Peabody books sitting by Jeff's bedside. I thought maybe I should get Jeff kidnapped and deprogrammed, but, since he was living at home, I supposed I couldn't do that. Dr. Osgood had no good advice to lay on me when I last saw her, and I was sure she wouldn't think this was an emergency now because no one was dying.

Since I was in solitary in my bedroom, I needed something to do. I took a shower and put on a t-shirt and PJ bottoms. It was early to go to bed, but I surely wasn't going back down to the living room while Floyd and company were still there. I took out one of my spy novels, got under the covers, and tried to keep from thinking about what was going on below me.

After they left, I heard Jeff call up from the stairwell.

"Melody. Come down. Let's talk."

This sounded ominous. What was happening to my Jeff?

He was waiting for me in the kitchen. He was still skinny, although less alarmingly so.

"Sit."

I obeyed.

"First, I have to apologize. We didn't mean to make you feel uncomfortable. We had just been in a rather intense discussion, and you took us by surprise."

Okay. I'd take that apology.

"Anyway, the Church advises members that communication with one's spouse is key to a successful marriage."

No kidding. They came up with that all by themselves?

"I understand this is all new to you, but you're not even trying. I've left many books in the house so you could learn about the teachings. You haven't picked up one of them."

He had to be kidding. I couldn't have spoken if I tried.

"I don't expect you to embrace the teachings as I have, but for us to communicate, I think it would be helpful if you knew what the teachings are."

I held back the urge to strangle him. Mr. Secretive, Mr. Non-Disclosure, lecturing me on communication. I reminded myself that he, too, was new at this. I had to give it a chance. It could work out. I doubted it, but I tried to remain hopeful. My Jeff was in there somewhere. I had to find him.

He sat there smiling like a Stepford wife, waiting for an answer.

I said, "Okay."

The last thing I wanted to do was read Philomathics

books. However, since I had promised, Saturday morning, after my run, I picked up the first book Jeff had brought in the house, *Philomathics and You*, and sat in the porch room to do some serious reading.

The book was filled with terminology and explanations and rules and — wow, I got lost in the first dozen pages. There was something called the "Pathway to Liberation," which I guessed was what they were calling the process of being enlightened. And I thought I already understood the meaning of *dekan*. Kind of like a soul, but more independent. It ruled the body. Or it created the body? I guess I wasn't clear on that after all. I went back and reread the chapter from the beginning. It was heartening to hear that they embraced people's families, because if it ended up that I wasn't good at this, maybe I wouldn't lose Jeff.

"How're you doing?"

He surprised me, and I jumped. He had slunk up to the porch room using his sock-covered, furtive, panther feet.

I decided to be honest.

"I'm kind of lost. I've started reading from the beginning again."

"That's fine. You'll get it. It'll come to you."

He smiled like one of those buddhas who was surrounded by bags of money.

"Thank you. I'll keep at it."

And he was gone. I heard music begin to play from the other room; it sounded like the band Fun.

I read another hour, and I had to accept one serious fact: I was hating this. Maybe it was because I felt I was forced into reading it. Maybe it was because I felt my husband had been highjacked. Or maybe, just maybe, it was because I didn't buy a word of it.

There was something called an *assessment*, which, as far as I could tell, was about removing past pain and suffering, so kind of like therapy. Anyway, Jeff admitted to me that he had already had several of these assessments, and they were helping him. He also said he had started working for the center, so he was getting his assessments for free. This terrified me. Would he become even more detached from himself, and from me?

Wait a minute: Assessments weren't ordinarily free?

On Sunday afternoons, he went to services, so, on one of those Sundays, I arranged to go into work. While Anton had not hired a new Art Director in my absence, he had hired some new hot-shot designer named, get this, Breezie, who relocated here from Florida, right out of college. I'm sure they were paying her nothing, but she was sticking her nose in everyone's projects, imposing herself on the picnic like a horsefly. I figured I could avoid her if I came in on the weekend.

I turned on my iPhone to play some work music: Julian Bream, Concerto Aranjuez by Joaquin Rodrigo. It was wonderful to have the whole office to myself with nothing to concentrate on but how this chair would go with that desk and if the colors and the lines looked right to me. I was trying something different, something Tamara, Laura, and I had discussed, and I told them I'd see what I could come up with over the weekend.

"Hi, Melody!"

Breezie. I swore, I couldn't catch a break. She came up

to my desk and put her fancy designer purse down on my drawings. Her long, black hair was held back with a glitter headband, and when she moved her head, her silky mane twitched back and forth like a serpent's tail. She had seven gold dangling bracelets on her right arm, and a rose-gold watch on her left. I was startled and confused, and when she reached over and turned off my music, I wanted to chew her hand off. Then she said, "Anton asked me to help you out with your project. I thought I'd come in and surprise you so we could get started right away."

I wanted to growl, "I don't like surprises," but I held my tongue.

I'm sure Anton didn't ask her to help me. I didn't need help with my work, and I certainly didn't need help from her. On the other hand, he must have told her I'd be in on Sunday. Had Anton joined the secret enemy forces that were currently destroying my life? Was this a kind of conspiracy the gods were concocting to teach me some kind of lesson?

She sat across from me and said, "So. Show me what you've got."

It would be a cold day in Death Valley before I shared my project with this carpetbagger, but I didn't know how to stall her. I hadn't had a chance to confront Anton. I was trapped.

I decided the safe thing would be to show her something that was close to being finished. Maybe she would do less damage.

"Okay. These are my drawings for the master. The wardrobes have—"

"The master?"

Good grief. "Bedroom... Anyway, the wardrobes have

34

vertical panels that match the headboards and footboards of the bed. Everything has a gray stain that lets the wood grain show through. And this is the mood board, with potential fabric swatches for the curtains and rugs. The different textures add visual interest, as do the pops of orange and yellow contrasting with the rich blues and purples of the bed linens. Take a look and see what you think."

She didn't stop that condescending smile as she looked everything over. She studied each piece, uttering, "Mm hm, mm hm...." Finally, she put everything down and said, "Don't you think we can do better than this?"

Okay. It was me against the world. Jeff was captured by aliens, Anton had betrayed me, and everything I knew about my life was changing. When I got home and found I was alone, I went into the music room and switched on the lamp. I picked out a Beatles CD, turned up the volume, and when the shuffled CD started at "Hello, Goodbye," I burst into tears.

I know. I said the Beatles made me happy. That wasn't always working these days. Thing was, my crying didn't necessarily mean I was sad. It could also mean I was frustrated. Or angry. Or homicidal.

Jeff returned about halfway through the CD. I was bawling, and I couldn't stop in time for him not to see it. He looked at me quizzically, and I paused the music.

"Is everything all right?" He seemed genuine, like himself; the way he was supposed to be.

What was I going to say? Yes? I'm crying my eyes out

because everything is fine? I'm crying because you're turning into an android? Because everything's changing and I have no control over it? I thought about it. "Office politics. I try so hard not to be involved, but suddenly I am." He was looking at me like this was not enough, so I added, "I'm seriously frustrated."

There was that real, kind, Jeff smile. "You'll be okay. You always are. You're the most talented designer in the place."

"Thank you."

"You know, you're thinking impulsively. If you start learning to think rationally, you might feel better."

At first, I thought he was being misogynistic, but then I realized this was from those books. The term they used for a gut reaction was an "impulsive." I held it together. I forced a laugh. "Like Mr. Spock?"

Real Jeff would have laughed. This Jeff beamed. "Yes. Something like that," he said. "I'm not good at explaining it; it's better that you read about it yourself. Then you can really absorb the meaning."

I calmed down enough to explain Anton's act of deception, and Jeff listened intently. Then he said, "It's not actually betrayal. He's acting rationally; he's keeping his employees busy. And Breezie is behaving rationally because she just wants to make the best product..."

"No, she wants to get ahead. She could give a damn about the product."

He smiled. "Okay. Get ahead. Still, rational."

I was not happy with this explanation. I didn't like having my feelings dismissed as irrational. I wasn't against Philomathics on the face of it, but to give a mentally ill person an entirely new way of thinking, was that really helping him? Or was it going to change him into someone I no longer recognized?

Now, I had something to say about me to Dr. Osgood: The world against Melody. Not too paranoid, was it?

I got to her office early. There were few magazines in the waiting room that I cared to read, although she was keeping a nice selection of *National Geographics* there. They usually amused me, even if it was just to look at pictures of animals. Before I picked one up, though, her door opened.

Dr. Osgood was older than I was, and she always dressed in a suit, which some days made me feel downright juvenile in comparison. Her hair, which was blond and cropped, was being held back by her glasses. As she sat down, she slid the readers back onto her nose, and her hair fell back down to frame her face. She couldn't read anything without her glasses, so she either kept them on her face or poised on her head.

She listened without interrupting me. After I finished my tirade about Sunday and Breezie, I related what Jeff said about my "impulsive" response.

"I know that's the Church, not him," I said, "but it's making me worried about what he might turn into."

She looked at me over her glasses.

"Did he tell you to read about it yourself? That you'd understand it better?"

"Actually, yes."

"I'm just going to give you something to think about."

"Okay."

"And I'm going to say this in the most non-biased way I can."

"Okay..."

"A big part of Philomathics is to get members to recruit people. It seems to me, you are being recruited."

"Me? Recruited?"

"Jeff got you to start reading the books, right?"

Well....

"It'll just be a matter of time before they expect more of you," she said. "I'm going to say this, not only as your therapist, but as a friend. Be careful."

3

My home office, like the rest of my house, was about 80% furnished by IKEA. Oh, there were a couple of pieces by West Elm and Wayfair here and there, mostly in the living room, but the office was almost all the Swedish modern look. I had a desk with clean lines and built-in drawers, and then a two-tone office chair, also from IKEA, that cost more than the desk, but was beautiful and really comfortable. I put a bench in front of the window that had a nice woven-cloth, cushioned top, and there was a white tube floor lamp brightening up the space. It wasn't a big room, but it functioned well as an office.

I was sitting at my desk reading *Philomathics and You* when Marie called. She was not taking this Philomathics business lying down. While Jeff and I were busy reading every word E. W. Peabody ever put to paper, she was researching the organization itself, becoming more driven as the days passed. This was all she could think of to help her son. And I couldn't do much of my own research, as I was busy being indoctrinated.

"Be careful," she said.

Hm. Not the first time I'd heard that.

"What did you find out?"

"They have a reputation for going after people who disagree with them. I know you are doing this for Jeff, but I think these people are very powerful. And dangerous."

"Going after... what does that entail?"

"Various kinds of harassment. People following you, people coming to your house, people calling you, that sort of thing."

"Well, I don't think they'll be coming after Jeff and me. We have nothing. We have no money. We have no power. We have no voices. We're minor players."

"From your lips to God's ears," she said.

After I hung up, my curiosity brought me back to the internet. I found this, again from Wikipedia:

> "The Church of Philomathics labels any critic of their organization a *Contrary Person*, a state of being which is considered dangerous and amoral. The Church has a reputation for hostile actions toward such defamers. A Philomathist who is in contact with a Contrary Person is referred to as a *Prospective Nuisance*.... This includes involvement with any Contrary Groups, such as members of the medical or mental health professions."

Dr. Osgood was a Contrary Person? That couldn't be right. That would mean that, because of me, they might view Jeff as one of these Prospective Nuisances. I read further:

"An individual in communication with a CP is considered unstable. This condition would potentially undermine any studies or treatments the individual might receive. Therefore, the individual will not be allowed to participate in much of the Philomathics training until the situation has been satisfactorily remedied."

"Satisfactorily remedied," how? I wasn't sure what they would do, and it scared me. Might Jeff be encouraged to distance himself from me so that he wouldn't be a threat to them? He used to love me more than anything, but now that he was ill, would he find the Church more important than his own wife?

I was a paranoid mess.

I had been instinctively hiding my disdain for the Church, and after talking to Marie, I realized what a good idea that was. I was sure they already mistrusted me. I was some weird hybrid, wife of a Philomathist, not the real thing. But I was worried about Jeff. How would he ever extract himself from this Church without angering them? It wasn't good to get a powerful organization mad at you, no matter who they were.

Dr. Osgood was not wrong about one thing. Jeff came home one night and brought Floyd with him. They sat me down in our living room like I was a child.

"We need to discuss your advancements in our teachings," Floyd said. Even up close, he had that glass-eyed look, staring right through me as if I were made of cellophane.

I looked at Jeff. He was smiling that other-worldly smile. And he said, "What Floyd is saying is that he'd like to invite you to the center to have an assessment."

There it was. It was time to get the wife to sign on. I looked from Jeff to Floyd and kept thinking about Prospective Nuisances and Contrary Persons. Would the simple act of not joining cause them to distrust me? Would the Church declare me a Contrary Person and encourage Jeff to pull away from me?

Although there was a little voice inside me repeating, "Don't do it," I found myself saying: "Okay. What do I do?"

Floyd's expression didn't change. "Come to the center. There is an introductory package that includes an anxiety test, plus your initial assessment, for $200."

I wanted to say, "So I have to pay to join this Church?" but I kept my cynicism to myself.

We had dinner with Floyd, a meal I had put together for Jeff and me. There was enough, but I was hoping for leftovers. They spent a lot of time discussing me, how good it would be for our marriage for me to join them. *My marriage was just fine before you came around, Floyd, you sanctimonious ass.* And I had news for him; I wasn't joining anything. I'd do their stupid assessment, and I'd read a book or two.

After Floyd left, Jeff turned to me.

"Feel like going upstairs?"

Upstairs? Upstairs, upstairs? Like, let's get physical, upstairs?

I couldn't believe it. It had been months. He started to climb the steps, then looked behind him to see if I was following. I quickly got up from the table and, after tripping on the first step and somehow falling up, scrambled to the bedroom, kicking my shoes off at the top of the staircase. He started to unbutton my shirt, and when

I tried to remove his, he said, "No. This is all about you."

He finished undoing my blouse, and it fell to the floor. Moving in closer, he gently caressed my arms, planting small kisses all over my neck. I leaned in against him, hoping to convey urgency, but when I tried again to touch him, he took hold of my wrists and put them behind me. The moonlight coming in the windows was in my eyes, so I closed them, and I relinquished all control. He let go of my wrists, and his hand moved behind me to unhook my bra. As he pressed against me, his clothes rubbed delightfully against my bare skin. I opened my eyes. He reached for my skirt, which he unzipped, and when it dropped around my ankles, I obediently stepped out of it. Last went my pantyhose. I felt so vulnerable, being undressed as I was, with him fully clothed. He picked me up, and placed me on the bed, kissing my forehead, then working his way down to my neck, my breasts, my waist, then he ran his hands up and down my legs.

With one hand, he started to undress. Soon his velvety skin was all over me. When he entered me, the rush was almost too much; it had been so long. I was staring into those green eyes, and I saw Jeff. The real Jeff. There he was.

When WXLI changed their format to sports talk, they decided to keep some music on the weekends. They offered Jeff a slot on Saturdays on the overnight. The catch was: he had to use their playlist, and it was all slow R&B, which Jeff dubbed, "fuck music." Saturday at midnight; what else would they want him to play? It wasn't so much that Jeff wouldn't play their list. He just thought he'd be bored. The playlist didn't have anything recorded before 2010; Jeff said it all sounded the same. He thought about it quite a while before he finally said no. It was very few hours, anyway. He assumed he'd find something else.

And when he couldn't find something else, he joined a cult.

The Church of Philomathics center was situated in an immense modern building that used to be a vacant lot. When it was first under construction, they brought in large clear slabs of glass, and I thought they were building an Apple store. The front entrance had a brick façade, but when I went through the doors, there was a space-age interior. The staff, dressed in navy jackets and robin's-egg blue ties or scarves, looked like airline stewards. They were extremely engaging and eager to please. The average salesperson could learn a lot from them. They almost made me want to shout, "Yes! Yes! Give me the $4,000 package!"

Yes, there was a $4,000 package.

Floyd and I took a glass elevator to the eighth floor, and he showed me to a room that would have been private, except that it was also made of glass. He explained to me that the first step would be for me to take the anxiety test, to see where I was. I suspected Floyd knew I was an imposter, but I wasn't sure he cared. He probably believed in the power of the teachings that, eventually, the Church would win me over.

Also, he had my $200.

Floyd introduced me to the psych device, a strange metal box with lots of plastic knobs and a gauge. I was to grab onto the handle, and it would read my anxiety apex.

I could have told him my anxiety apex was at an all-time high without the machine.

"Jeff tells me you're full of emotions these days. You haven't been happy. Tell me about it. Just talk as you normally would."

He was writing down everything I was saying. What was he going to do with this information? Were they going to store it somewhere? And why? I smartly didn't blurt out everything I was thinking, like, "Fuck you, Floyd, give me my Jeff back!" He started to ask me all of these questions about Jeff, about our life together, about our relationship, about our sex life. I was so worried that I would tell him something that would give me away that I started crying. I was too nervous. I was going to lose Jeff to these people, and I had no power to stop it.

Sure enough, I failed the anxiety test. All impulsive, no rationale.

"This is excellent," Floyd said. "We've made a good start."

"Thank you," I said. I thought thanking him was a good touch, even though I felt humiliated at letting this snake see me cry. If he knew I was hating this, he didn't let on.

The assessment itself was tedious. Floyd used the same machine, that psych device, and told me to close my eyes and think of the most recent thing I could think of that upset me, something I wouldn't mind sharing. I wanted to say, "You mean this, right now?" but decided instead to pick the day Jeff met Floyd, those hours when I was so worried about him. I explained the day, the parts I thought were accurate, and then Floyd said, "Okay. Now tell me, again, adding more details."

I sighed and repeated myself, trying to add more

information. I think I was making up most of it, but Floyd wouldn't know that. After three or four tries at this, he had me think of something older but comparable; again, something I didn't mind imparting.

"Something comparable?" I had to think a minute. "Okay. When Jeff first got depressed, before it had gotten really bad, he took the car out to run some errands. He was gone for hours. I didn't think anything of it at the time, because he often would take a drive, hit some record stores, things like that. But then I got a call from a hospital. Police had found him unresponsive, sitting in his car. The hospital tested him for drugs, but when they found none, they called me. He had perked up by then, so they told him to see his doctor and let him go home."

When I was through relating this, Floyd had me repeat myself again. And again. And again. I mean, what difference did it make what he was wearing, or what I was wearing, or exactly the time of day? I honestly didn't understand the point of this exercise, and I was getting hungry. Finally, he said, "Okay. Now think of a pleasant memory. It can be something simple."

First thing that came to mind was sex with Jeff, but I sure as hell wasn't going to recount our private lives to anybody, especially not to this replicant. I chose feeding the birds. That seemed to satisfy him, and he said he was going to count to three and say, "Replaced," and I could open my eyes.

Wow. I felt a little hypnotized from trying to remember details, but otherwise, what a load of bear dung. Again, if this was helping Jeff, how bad could it be? I was probably just doing it wrong.

Then there were the services. An hour or more of some

Philomathist reading from E. W. Peabody's books. Even dead, this master mentalist was a blustering blowhard. If I wanted to go to a church, I'd go to a real one. Besides, I didn't understand how they even got church status. So far, they hadn't mentioned God once. I should have declared myself a church and gotten tax-exempt status too.

Of course, I had to keep these opinions to myself. This was something that was helping Jeff. I had to learn to refrain from talking about things I knew little about.

Monday morning, Anton called me into his office.

"So.... How's Breezie working out?"

I didn't trust Breezie as far as I could throw her, but I played along. I liked my job.

"Well, I would have appreciated a heads up that I'd be working with her."

Anton laughed. "You always were direct. I like that. Yes, I'm sorry; I should have told you she asked me if she could be on a project with you. I didn't know she would take it upon herself to join you last Sunday."

Men were so stupid about women, it made me want to spit.

"Did everything go okay?"

"After the initial shock, yes. We can work together. I can work with anybody."

"Good. I'm glad that my two star people will be working together," he said.

I was tempted to ask him how this twenty-something newbie got to be one of his star people, but I could figure that out for myself. She was pretty. She was pushy. She was young. She was conniving.

"The reason I've called you in here: I have a new project for you. The Maplewood Company would like us to create a new line for their fall series. I thought this was something you should take lead on. And I've asked Breezie and Evelyn to be on your team."

"Okay. That's fine."

"Good. I'll call a meeting with the client."

I wasn't sure what Breezie would have to contribute, but at least I had Evelyn, who, like me, was a senior designer. Evelyn and I hadn't worked together much over the years. This should be interesting.

I got home early for a change, but the lights were out in the house, so Jeff wasn't there yet. He probably had walked over to the gym. I went for a run. Maybe we'd have chicken tonight. I felt like cooking.

I took an extra-long run, then went grocery shopping, and when I got home, the house was still dark.

"Hello?"

That was odd. Jeff should've been home by now. It was like the days when Jeff was.... Oh, no.

I ran up the stairs. Jeff was down again.

"Jeff?"

"I'm sorry Melody. I'm just not feeling up to it."

That was how he said, "I'm depressed. Leave me alone."

"Can I call someone? Want to talk to my therapist?"

He didn't answer right away. Then he said, "Could you call Floyd?"

Floyd and his airline-steward cronies arrived in minutes and went up the stairs. They were in our bedroom for hours, doing I don't know what. At this point, I would have called an exorcist if it would get Jeff out of bed again. I had been ignoring the fact that Jeff was still ill. He had seemed so much better; not himself, exactly, but better. Now he was down again.

It was the middle of the night when they left. Jeff was still in bed, but he smiled when he saw me.

"I'm a little tired now. Can we talk in the morning?"

I said of course. He looked better. He sounded better. It remained to be seen if he stayed better.

I spent the rest of the night watching him sleep. By sunrise, I was finally nodding off and realized there was no way I'd be productive at work. I called in sick.

Around noon, Jeff woke me up.

"Hey, Melody."

I opened my eyes to see Jeff fully dressed, with that strange smile, holding a cup of coffee. He offered it to me and sat on the bed.

"I think today I'm going to look for a job."

"What? Really? That's...uh...great." Here was a person who took to his bed yesterday and was now talking about job hunting. I sipped some coffee before I responded. "Doing what? Have you decided yet?"

"No. I'm just going to see what's available."

I drank some more coffee. This surreal morning started coming into focus.

"Okay. Well, do you need anything from me?"

"No. Just wanted to tell you."

With that, he went downstairs. I could hear music start playing: Motown. Jeff's recovery seemed to be taking hold.

I rolled back over for another hour, then got up to go run. When I got home, he was still in the music room, busily searching job possibilities on his iPad.

What did they do to him, anyway? I could tell he was not all there. But yes, up was better than down.

On Sunday, Jeff went to the gym, and then he was probably going over to the center for services. I settled into my home office to work on my current design project. Breezie had been questioning everything Evelyn and I came up with, and if I wanted to work without her, it had to be at home. I guessed I really didn't work well with others. Well, her, anyway.

At least, so far, she didn't know where I lived.

The doorbell rang. Oh crap. Did I conjure her up?

It was Floyd.

"Hi, Floyd. Jeff is at the gym."

"I know," he said. "I came over to talk to you."

It occurred to me that maybe Floyd was like a vampire: once invited in, he'd be in to stay. Despite my better judgement, I let him in. We sat down in the living room, and he stared right through me with that robot glare of his. It took him a ridiculously long time to start talking.

"We feel you are falling behind on your studies."

My studies? What, were they going to give me a test?

"We know you're doing this for Jeff. We find that very commendable. As you know, families are very important to Mr. Peabody."

I wanted to say, "Mr. Peabody is dead," but Marie said the Church actually believed he was somehow among us, so I held my tongue.

"However, if you are resistant to the teachings, you won't learn."

How did he know I was resistant? I swallowed my pride and said, "So what should I do?"

He smirked at me, which I believe was supposed to be a kindly smile.

"Do more reading. Especially hone up on the terminology."

I had been blipping over the weird words they made up, like when you read a book that has a lot of foreign names.

He continued. "I know you like to listen to music, but I think it would be better if it's quiet when you read."

How did he know... anything? What was Jeff telling him? I said, "Okay."

"Also, you like to run. Instead of music, we have Mr. Peabody's works recorded. You can listen to them on your iPhone."

He smirked at me again, and said, "Okay?"

I didn't think I could answer with anything else. I said, "Okay."

"You know that not keeping up with your studies will impede Jeff's development as well. We wouldn't want that, now, would we?"

I shook my head.

"Good. I'll come back another time to evaluate your progress." He stood up. "That is all."

I shut the door behind him. If I thought I was going to skate through this, I was mistaken. I waited a moment to make sure he was gone. Then I went into the music room, found Blondie's first album, and cranked up the volume.

Before we moved to Floral Park, we were living in an apartment in Garden City. Most of our things, like Jeff's albums, were stored in the basement of the building. Marie and Frank had offered to hold them for us at their house in North Valley Stream, but no matter where our things were stored, we didn't have easy access to them. We needed a house.

We decided to bring Marie along with us when we went to look at houses. So far, she hadn't liked anything we had seen. We had to agree; nothing had seemed right yet, although our reasons had been different than hers. Hers were more practical. Ours were gut reactions.

From the outside, the Floral Park house appeared to be a good size, maybe because there was no yard to speak of. I fell in love with the picture window immediately.

"This looks nice," I said.

"There's no yard," Marie said helpfully. "And it's a used house. There might be too many things to fix."

Jeanine, who was our broker, respectfully held her tongue about that.

"Yeah, the yards in this neighborhood are small," she said. "By the way, that's my house next door." We looked over at her place as she opened the door to this one. Her house was maybe 12 feet away from the one we were seeing. There were perfect evergreen hedges along the perimeter of the yard, and it seemed to be sitting on a larger piece of land. The one we were about to see had the picture window, though.

The previous occupants had already moved out, so I

could get a clear idea of how I would furnish the place. I loved the size and shape of the living room; the house had good bones. I was mentally putting the couch, probably something from Wayfair, in the middle of the room. The television would go on the side away from the window, some nice lamps from West Elm on either side, one of my mother's paintings in the foyer...

"Look. There's a built-in window seat," Jeff said. I had been taken by the outside of the picture window, he by the inside.

"Yes, that's a nice feature," Jeanine said. "The previous owners added that right after they moved in."

Jeff sat in the window and grinned. "This is great."

"There's a full bath, through the door to the left of the kitchen," Jeanine said. "There are also two small bedrooms on this level. The master bedroom and bath are upstairs."

Jeff wandered off to look at the far bedroom. I followed him.

"Are you thinking record storage?" I said.

"Yeah. The house does have three bedrooms. You wouldn't mind, would you?"

"No, it's a perfect place for that. We could put a guestroom in the other one."

"Or an office for you...."

As we exited the room, Jeanine said, "The two bedrooms down here are about the same square footage, slightly different footprints."

Marie was looking in the kitchen, and we followed her. Jeanine continued her running commentary:

"The kitchen is an average size for this area. There's a dining alcove to the left, and a small closed-in porch room off the back of the house."

We all collected back in the center of the living room and stared at her.

"Ready to see upstairs?"

Hell, Jeff and I were ready to move in...

...but upstairs clinched it. It was a good-sized bedroom. There were windows along the front wall, and the room was flooded with sunlight. Once we moved in, we spent a lot of our time trying to keep the sun out of the room because of the heat, but on first glance, we were wowed. Even Marie was impressed.

"Is there room to park two cars?" she said. Impressed, but still not completely convinced. "The kids have two cars."

"One in the driveway, and there's parking on the street," Jeanine said. "There is also a small but nice backyard I'll show you when we get back downstairs."

Jeff was off inspecting the shower, which was a big and fancy with an oversized showerhead. He came back into the bedroom, and announced, "I want to live here."

We laughed, but we all knew he was serious.

While Jeff was upstairs taking another shower, I was in the porch room, again trying to make some sense out of *Philomathics and You*. It was getting a little cold to be sitting out there, but I was wearing one of Jeff's sweaters, so I felt warm and secure. Since Floyd had reprimanded me the other day that my understanding of the material was subpar, I had agreed to do better. Now, I was hating this even more.

Jeff walked up to the glass porch-room door wearing

his robe.

He grinned. "Come upstairs with me?"

I threw the book down and scampered up the stairs after him. He was standing by the bed, and when he opened his arms to hug me, his robe fell open. I took a moment to gaze at his body. The honey-colored hair on his torso was fluffy and curly, and I ran my hands over his chest, his thighs, all over. His skin felt so smooth and warm, I just wanted to rub against him all night. He gave me a long passionate kiss, and then started chewing on my neck. I managed to take off the sweater and my bra, and then reached behind him to put my hands on his butt to pull him closer. I was practically panting when he held my face up to his and said, "I think we should have children."

"Uh... what?" I was too aroused to talk, but this was definitely destroying the mood. As he kissed my breasts, he said again: "I... think... we... should... have... children."

I would have agreed to do anything at that point, but there were some reality issues getting in the way. First, I had an IUD, so there would be no baby making tonight no matter what I agreed to. Second, we were both in our forties. We shouldn't become parents without careful consideration. And third, and most importantly, I didn't want to have children, even with Jeff.

He grabbed me tighter and kissed me hard. I struggled out of the rest of my clothes and we lay on the bed. He whispered in my ear, "So what do you say?"

I looked into his eyes. Was this really Jeff? Was this the Church speaking through Jeff? Was this the mental illness taking some new form? I wanted sex, not babies, and I wanted it right now.

Before I could answer, he kissed me again, softer this

time, and said, "It's okay. We'll talk about it in the morning."

I was afraid he was going to leave me there, wanting him, but, although he was ill, he would never be mean. I closed my eyes, and savored every caress, every movement, every bit of him.

We were a couple who never wanted a family. We were a couple who loved our respective jobs. We were a couple who loved to come home to each other at night. For years, that was enough.

The next morning, I opened my eyes, and Jeff was watching me.

"Jeff?" I sat up.

"Melody.... I'm sorry. For last night. Children. We agreed we didn't want them. I'm sorry I brought it up. That wasn't me."

"Well...who was it?"

"The Church...Floyd...encourages couples to have kids."

"You remember I have an IUD, right?"

"Yes, of course. I'm sorry."

"Okay."

He wasn't giving me that bizarre grin. He was looking me in the eye, and I felt something different from him, something I hadn't seen much since he joined the Church. He was being... genuine.

4

When Jeff was first hired at WXLI, they wanted him to think of some type of event to herald in his arrival. He suggested they announce an all-request Saturday, where he would be the DJ all day. The station told him that would be too hard. They were an AOR station. What if someone asked for something from the 50s?

"Doesn't matter. I'm only going to play one song, no matter what they ask for. They can ask for Frank Sinatra, they'll still get the same thing."

They liked the idea.

He had a week to prepare for this event. He decided he had to pick the one song carefully. It had to be something annoying, but fun.

He chose "Chirpy Chirpy Cheep Cheep," by Mac and Katie Kissoon.

"This is Jeff Hollenback, coming to you on WXLI, broadcasting from the beautiful pineapple capital of the world, Garden City, Long Island. Welcome to our all-request Saturday. Yes, you can request anything: any song, from any decade."

The phones lit up. People were requesting everything from the Moonglows to Megadeth. They only got one song, though.

"Requested by Steve from Oyster Bay. From Led Zeppelin's untitled fourth album, also known as Led Zeppelin IV, 'Stairway to Heaven.'"

And he'd play "Chirpy Chirpy Cheep Cheep."

The event was a great success. People were calling all day, at first, to try to request songs. Jeff would always give a fact or a piece of trivia about each song. He just wouldn't play it. As the realization sunk in as to what was really going on, people would call just to talk. Some tried to stump him by picking something really obscure to see if he could come up with some information about it. Some would actually request "Chirpy Chirpy Cheep Cheep." Jeff managed to keep everyone entertained, using one song, for 24 hours. It was brilliant.

I was thinking about that as I ran with my stupid E. W. Peabody audiobook playing on my iPhone. I would have liked nothing better than to be listening to "Chirpy Chirpy Cheep Cheep," over and over, instead. I ran into the park and headed for the pond, with the words of E. W. Peabody droning on in my ears, and the late-fall air turning the exposed part of my face into a chapped mess. I noticed there were no birds, no humans, nothing except me and the disembodied words of Mr. Peabody, a man who, I had concluded by now, was an egomaniacal nutcase.

Even though it was a ridiculous song, when I got home, I found "Chirpy Chirpy Cheep Cheep" on one of Jeff's CDs (a collection of 70s "hits") and turned up the volume.

Floyd was taking a special interest in me. (Oh, joy.) He would show up at the house at random times to quiz me on the teachings. How could I make him leave me alone, and not have him figure out that I hated him, hated the Church, and, especially, hated E. W. Peabody? The thing was, there was nothing in Philomathics I could find that was like, say, the Beatitudes. There was no poetry, no profundity, no hymns, no comfort. It was pure, insane, bullshit. Never mind that Mr. Peabody didn't have an original thought in his head. Everything was based on something else. A dekan was essentially a soul — a soul from another planet, but a soul. Past lives were a Buddhist concept. The Church had services like other churches did, assessments were like therapy, purges were their form of rehab, the stupid Pathway to Liberation was like Nirvana. (Also, Stairway to Heaven. Ha, "buying a stairway to heaven." Most appropriate for this cult.) Except it was really all about power. The further one went along the Pathway, the more power one had over his situations, other people, and, of course, in the organization.

And the more money the Church would accumulate.

Jeff, meanwhile, still insisted on keeping his hair short. Not sure what that was about, although I was pretty sure it had something to do with the Church. Lately he had been spending a lot of time sitting by the picture window, staring. This was how his depression originally started, and it had me worried. On the days he spent by the window, I'd call in late and sit with him. Sometimes he'd talk. Sometimes he would smile at me and say nothing. Sometimes, he'd stand up, and either go to the gym, or take a shower and come get me so we could make love. I had him partially back, but it was disconcerting.

There was one whole weekend where he was acting pretty normal—Church normal, not pre-depression normal—so I could relax a little and not worry as much. It was such a relief that, on Monday, I got to the office early to catch up on my work. My desk was cleared of all of my sketches. I stood there, befuddled, and heard Anton's voice behind me.

"Melody? Can we talk?"

"What's going on?"

"Come into my office."

He closed the door.

"I've taken you off as lead designer on the Maplewood Project. I know you've been having trouble at home and thought you could do without that pressure."

When I found my voice, I said, "And you made Breezie lead, right?"

"Well, she knows the project better than anyone, besides you. I knew you wouldn't trust anyone else."

Again: Men. Are. Clueless.

"What about Evelyn?" I said.

"Breezie has worked with you more recently."

It was true that Evelyn and I didn't pair up very often. Still...

"Evelyn has more experience."

"Don't worry. Breezie can handle it."

Thank you for ignoring my concerns, Boss. "So, Evelyn and I, who are both senior designers, report to Breezie?"

He smiled. "That's right."

There were so many things about this that were wrong; I couldn't speak. And if I was upset, Evelyn must have been livid. I stood up to leave.

"I hope things get better at home," he said. "We're all pulling for you."

I tried not to look completely miserable as I walked out of his office. Cursing and yelling, while warranted, would not send the right message. I ran right into Breezie on my way back to my desk. She gave me a gloating smirk. That little grifter. She was behind this. The fact that I was on to her was of no solace.

I didn't even feel like running when I got home. I sat in the music room, in the dark, in silence, and pouted. I knew what Floyd would say, that I was having "an impulsive." And Dr. Osgood would ask, "How does that make you feel?"

I wanted to punch something. To break something. To wring something with my bare hands until it choked to death.

The doorbell rang.

Floyd, you have got to be kidding me.

It had to be him. He knew one of us was home because the car was in the driveway, and he knew it was me, because he probably knew where Jeff was. I just couldn't answer the door. *Maybe I'm out running, Floyd. Maybe I'm taking a bath. Maybe I'm sitting in the dark, by myself, hoping you'll go away.*

He rang the bell again. When I didn't answer that time, he looked in the window. From where I sat, I could see the white tufts of hair that protruded from his stupid oblong head, but I didn't think he could see me. Although normally one could see right through the double-wide doorway into the room, I was sitting in one of the large sofa chairs with the lamp off. Whether he saw me or not, he finally went away.

Maybe that was how to get rid of Floyd. Ignore him.

I felt oddly content, sitting in Jeff's music room, surrounded by thousands of silent LPs, CDs, and singles. I thought about when we were first dating and Jeff would take me into the City to see shows. We would see some of the craziest bands. (Liquid Tape Deck at Arlene's Grocery came to mind.) He'd make a running commentary, and the harder I laughed, the more inspired he'd be. If we liked the band, we would introduce ourselves. We'd get CDs and tapes, sometimes even vinyl. A lot of those unknown bands would end up on mix CDs Jeff made for friends' parties.

I was just heading upstairs to take a bath when I heard Jeff at the door.

"Hey Melody," he called. "Guess who I ran into?"

Floyd. He was a freaking boomerang.

Christmas was approaching; there were just two weeks to go. I hadn't even had time to think about it, and I was sure Jeff hadn't either. Philomathics allowed its members to celebrate whatever religious holidays they chose—as long as they also took Peabody's words as gospel. Not that I celebrated Christmas as a religious holiday, mistrusting organized religion as I did. But I did love Christmas. To me, it symbolized hope for the future. And these days, I could use all the hope I could get.

Jeff was in a pretty sane mood on Saturday, so I took a

chance and drove over to the mall. Parking was close to impossible. I found a space so far away from the stores I wished I had a bicycle. I wasn't sure when I would have this opportunity again, so I pulled into the spot and took the long walk across the parking lot.

Just entering the mall was difficult because of the hordes. I hadn't experienced that many people in my environs in a long time. I forced my way to the men's store first. The choices were expensive, and Jeff hadn't worn much besides t-shirts and jeans for quite a while now. What, I was going to buy him a $100 tie? A $175 (on sale) dress shirt that he'd never wear? This wasn't the place to buy something for Jeff.

There was a man standing just outside the men's shop, staring at his phone. I noticed him because he was wearing an incredibly ugly, loud, plaid jacket, a gray knit cap, and glasses so thick they looked like goggles. I was surprised they let him stand there. It wasn't exactly a good advertisement for their shop.

Dude, you really need to go in that store and buy yourself some decent clothes.

I was back in the torrent of shoppers. I found the bookstore, but that was a bust as well. I was getting worried. What did you get someone who was no longer interested in anything?

And then, I saw something great in the department store window. I rushed over, pushing past people to get in the store. This would be amazing if they still had it in stock.

Because of the lines, it took some time to make my purchase. The giftwrap line was lengthy as well, but since I hated wrapping gifts, I didn't mind waiting to have someone else do it for me. The other people in line had multiple packages, so I'd be there a while. I saw the guy in the ugly jacket get in line, holding a new sweater and a bag from that men's store. Guess he overheard my thoughts about his wardrobe.

I got home, and Floyd was sitting with Jeff in our living room.

"Hey, Melody. Look who's here?"

I'm sure the delight could be seen all over my face.

Breezie was now proving to everyone, except Anton, her true identity—a colossal, ever-smiling, she-devil. Since she had never bothered to learn how to use a computer, and she couldn't manually sketch a tic-tac-toe game, she had me rendering sketches, which is what we called creating virtual rooms on the computer. I usually liked doing that, but not instead of being involved in original concepts. It was intended to belittle me.

I was sitting at my desk on a Monday morning, practically enjoying doing grunt work so I wouldn't have to see Breezie's face. Someone mentioned to me that she was in the main conference room holding a meeting about the Maplewood Project (i.e., my project; no, I wasn't bitter), a meeting I wasn't told about. The client was there; so were Anton and Evelyn. I wasn't going to join the meeting late. That would look worse than just not showing up. There were other, smaller projects in the office; for instance, the one Tamara and Laura were on. I was thinking maybe I could catch Anton when their meeting let out and ask him if I could help out on one of those.

They were in there a long time, but eventually, everyone stopped talking and the door opened. I was watching out for Anton, when Breezie walked up to my desk. She put her hand on my shoulder, leaned down, and said, "Be a dear and get me some coffee?"

Okay. Now she was openly fucking with me. I was not going to make a scene, especially since Anton and the client were still in earshot. I was not going to be a victim, either, and I surely was not going to get her coffee.

I pondered my options.

"No," I said, calmly.

"What?" She was smiling smugly.

You don't need coffee. Your venom will keep you awake.

I got up and went to Anton's office and waited for him.

"Melody. There you are. We missed you at the meeting."

"Hmm, yeah. Never got the meeting email. You could have called me."

"Breezie wanted to get started. I thought you were just running late."

That was a pretty lame response. I was never late to meetings. I decided to appeal to his reasonable side, while I still thought he had one.

"Anyway, I was wondering if I could help out with any of the other projects in the office."

"But the Maplewood Project, that's your baby."

Yeah, my baby's been kidnapped.

"I know. I just think a smaller project might be less, you know, pressure."

I hated using Jeff as an excuse. I certainly hated it when other people did it. On the other hand, I needed to get away from Breezie.

Anton nodded.

"I understand. No problem. I'm sure we can find a place for you elsewhere. Let me talk to the other teams and get back to you."

Problem solved, for now, and I didn't have to throw Breezie off a bridge. Then I had an unpleasant thought: I had just acted rationally, instead of having an emotional reaction.

Good grief. Was all of this Philomathics bullshit seeping into my brain?

"I think I'm in trouble."

Dr. Osgood had time to see me over lunch. She was writing something and didn't look up.

"Go on," she said.

I hated when she said therapy phrases like that, but I needed to talk about this.

"I'm worried Philomathics is affecting the way I think."

She lifted her glasses to look at me.

"Well, you're here. That's not thinking like a Philomathist."

"But is it possible to be reading and listening to all of this stuff and not become one of them?"

"I'm sure you're absorbing some of the terminology. Doesn't mean you're thinking like them. You grew up studying Catholicism. Are you still Catholic?"

"Well, not really, no."

"And do you still hate E. W. Peabody?"

"Oh, yeah. I hope whatever planet they sent him to is

making him listen to tapes of his own nonsense over and over and over until he begs for mercy."

"Well, then, I think you're fine. You can't get brainwashed just by reading the materials. You have to either be open to it, which you're not, or actively be brainwashed, deprived of sleep and all the rest." She smiled. "How's Jeff?"

I could talk about Jeff?

"The same. Sometimes sitting in the living room staring out of the window, sometimes lifting weights, sometimes being trained, sometimes being assessed."

"What do you think these assessments are doing for him?"

"Not sure. He says they really help him. It's part of the Pathway to Liberation, which, as far as I can tell, is like their Nirvana. Only with psychic abilities and aliens."

Dr. Osgood thought a moment, and said, "Realize that Jeff is struggling. You say he doesn't seem like himself. He's been through a lot of changes lately, and don't forget, he's still not well. Philomathics is just a Band-Aid."

This made sense to me. I nodded.

"Okay. Now let's talk about you."

I returned to the office, feeling less like a Floyd clone. I sat at my desk, intending on doing some more computer rendering for Breezie's project. I didn't like to sit idly, and it might have taken Anton a while to find me a project. While I was working, an email came in from Evelyn:

"Melody—Can you stop by when you have a moment?"

Curious, I headed over to her side of the studio. She

looked around the office when she saw me and said, "Let's go outside. Grab your coat?"

Evelyn and I had never said much more than "What should we do for drapes?" to each other over the past eight years. I couldn't imagine what she had to say to me now.

We went down to the parking level and sat on the curb. Evelyn stretched her long legs out in front of her. She was a strangely angular woman. I imagined she must have been a child athlete; she was all bones and joints.

"That meeting you missed...." she started. My defenses went up. She must have seen it on my face because she said, "No. I know Breezie deliberately didn't tell you about it. We all know who the enemy is here."

I nodded. Now I understood why she wanted to talk to me.

"Anyway, you and I did all of that design work. All Breezie did was ask stupid questions and take notes. So, at the meeting, Breezie presented our work. She never once said 'we,' or more accurately, 'they.' It was only 'I.' And when she was done, Anton said to her, 'Nice job, Breezie.' As if you and I didn't exist."

Well, if I thought I was becoming a Philomathist, I was wrong. I was having an impulsive. There was no rational thinking involved.

"That little scorpion," I said. "Doesn't Anton know how much work we did?"

"He probably does. But in front of the client, it was all about her. When I left the conference room, everyone was congratulating her. Not one word about you, not one to me."

"Well, I suppose I should tell you. I just asked Anton to take me off the Maplewood project."

"What? Why?"

"I told him it was because of the pressure. But it's Breezie. I prefer not to be annoyed while I'm working."

Evelyn laughed.

"Great. You're leaving her with me."

"He'll replace me with someone. He'll have to."

"Well, he better. There needs to be some kind of buffer between me and her."

When I got home, Jeff greeted me with, "You don't really support the teachings yet, do you?"

Somehow, I was found out. I had tried to play it so cool.

"What do you mean?"

"You're still seeing your therapist."

My stupid therapist was going to get me outed?

"Well, yeah. If you haven't noticed, I'm still a mess."

"Okay, but you know how the Church feels about that. Psychologists and psychiatrists are Contrary Persons. We're not supposed to be in contact with them."

"I kind of knew they didn't believe in therapy. I didn't know it was verboten."

"Well, now you know." He sounded like a disappointed parent. "Why don't you schedule another assessment with Floyd? They really help me. They'll start helping you."

I hated stupid assessments. I hated having to be in a room one on one with that horrible Floyd, especially with him writing down everything I said. And then have to pay, now $400, for the privilege. With Floyd closely overseeing my development, it was like he could read my mind. Besides, Jeff actually believed Floyd was helping him. I needed to watch what I said.

Dr. Osgood had suggested I spend some of my free time with friends from work. I knew Laura was a runner, and she lived close by, actually in jogging distance. Even though it was a bit wintry, I asked her if she'd like to join me on my morning run on Saturday. She had already jogged to my house, but she was in her twenties, and I had trouble keeping up with her. Nevertheless, it was nice to have someone to talk to who didn't believe in the doctrine of E. W. Peabody.

We returned to the house, and I made some coffee.

"Wanna see the music room?"

The music room wasn't a large space, and with shelves on every wall, it left little room for furniture, just two sofa chairs and a floor lamp. The custom shelves were floor-to-ceiling, and made to spec: album shelves, CD shelves, even shelves for 45s. The stereo was perfectly balanced to the room; although, I could still hear the music when I wanted to dance around in the living room.

"Wow! This is amazing. You said Jeff used to be a DJ?"

"Yeah. The radio kind, not the I-play-records-at-parties-and-I'm-actually-the-star kind."

She laughed. Someone thought I was funny again. That was refreshing.

She walked around the room.

"This is an amazing collection. How many albums does he have?"

"It's probably around 5,000 LPs and CDs."

"Wow," she said. "What do you usually listen to?"

I was going to delve into my weird logic of what I play and when but decided to keep it simple.

"Mostly Beatles."

"Me too."

Interesting. A fifth-generation Beatles fan.

"Do you have a favorite album?" she said. "I like the White Album."

"Hmm. Maybe Abbey Road. Most people ask for a favorite song, which of course is impossible. Jeff always tells people that his favorite Beatles' song is 'Wild Honey Pie.'"

"'Wild Honey Pie'?" She laughed.

"Either people don't get it, or they know enough about the Beatles, and Jeff, and they laugh. It's actually my ringtone when he calls."

I wondered what his answer to that question would be these days. He'd probably say something like "The Long and Winding Road," and I'd have to divorce him.

"Melody, can I ask you something?"

"Sure."

"Just between you and me, what do you think of Breezie?"

I didn't hesitate. "The Devil's spawn."

"Oh," she said. "You see it too. Is that why you asked to be on our project?"

"Yes."

"She's really awful to me. I don't know what I did. I'm just a junior designer. I'm no threat to her."

"She's a sociopath. She doesn't like anyone who isn't going to promote her agenda. Just keep that in mind, and you'll be fine."

The doorbell rang.

"Oh crap," I said.

I switched off the lamp, but it was a sunny day, and there was light streaming in the windows.

"Shhh," I said.

"Who is it?" she whispered.

"Probably Floyd."

She looked at me questioningly, but I put my finger to my lips and then motioned to her to follow me to the back corner of the room. We crouched down. The doorbell rang again.

My view of the window was mostly blocked, but I could see the top of Floyd's balding head as he looked in.

"Who's Floyd?" she whispered.

"Jeff's bizarre friend from the Church of Philomathics."

We waited, hunkering down, until it seemed that he had gone. We slowly stood up, and I was about to turn the lamp back on, when I heard the front door opening. Did Floyd have a key?

"Melody?"

Jeff was home. Floyd was with him. In a moment of inspiration, I wrapped the corner of my shirt around my hand so I wouldn't burn my fingers, and then unscrewed the lightbulb from the lamp. Then Laura and I went into the living room.

"Hi, Jeff. Floyd, this is Laura. We were... just discussing work."

"In the dark?" Floyd was staring through me again but was showing displeasure.

You have your weird little rituals, I have mine.

I held up the lightbulb. "Bulb went out."

We stood in uncomfortable silence for another

moment, and then Jeff said, "Well, I'm sure you two have a lot to discuss. Floyd, why don't you and I go out and get some lunch?"

When they were gone, Laura said, "Ooh. Creepy."

"So, you see it too."

Jeff and I decided I should join his gym. This had two practical applications: I didn't have to run in the frigid weather, and I could spend more time with Jeff.

We were walking home together one evening, both of us shivering, but in good moods.

"Are you hungry?" I said. "Maybe we can order a pizza."

"That would be great. Hey," he said, "look at that."

It was a small rabbit, sitting in the middle of someone's lawn. He was white with black-tipped ears. This was unusual around here. Most of our rabbits were brown. I wondered if he was someone's pet.

"He looks like a baby. Do you think he's okay?" I said. "Why is he sitting so still?"

The rabbit was motionless. He looked like one of those puffball mushrooms. I guessed he decided we weren't interested in eating him because, after a few moments, he hopped away.

"I think he's okay," Jeff said. "He doesn't seem injured."

I looked up the rabbit on the internet when I got home. He was probably a snow-shoe hare. His fur would only be white in the winter, and, it being so close to Christmas, he was snowball-colored. When it got warmer, he'd turn brown, like the other rabbits, but he'd be bigger.

Christmas did bring some hope this year. I had completely forgotten they gave bonuses at work. It wasn't a crazy amount, but it was really going to help with the money I spent on Jeff's present, plus the money I had been spending to have the Church hypnotize me.

We didn't put up a tree, but I did buy a fresh wreath and hang it on the door. Jeff got up before I did Christmas morning and made us breakfast in bed. Later, we'd be heading over to his parents' house for dinner.

"Want to exchange gifts now?" he said.

"Sure."

He brought the trays downstairs, and I went to get his gift. We met by the picture window.

"You first," he said.

When did he have time to shop? I started to carefully undo the wrapping paper, but he said, "Just rip it."

It was a set of DVDs of the Mike Douglas show, the week when John and Yoko guest hosted.

"Mike Douglas let John and Yoko guest host for a whole week?" I said. "Was he insane?"

Jeff smiled. "I used to have this set on VHS, but then I saw the DVDs at one of my old haunts. They're hard to find."

"Wow... I've never seen this. I've never even heard of this."

"Do you like it?"

"Love it. Thank you." I kissed him. "Now yours."

"Okay."

The package was beautifully wrapped. The store did a great job. But away it went, ripped to pieces and thrown to the floor.

"Wow. Where did you get this?"

"Is it okay?"

It was a Turkish robe. The color, compared to his old robe, was very close. Matching an exact hue is impossible. Unless you're matching paint, you better be prepared to settle.

"It's... amazing."

He was smiling, an unadulterated, Jeff smile.

5

Sometime after Jeff and I moved in together, Jeff took me to a noise concert. We were in the City to see Alice Cooper, and later there was a noise band Jeff wanted to see playing in the East Village.

We had a lot of trouble finding the club. The door was painted black and was wedged between a laundromat and a deli. No sign, just a large man, also in black, standing by the entrance, checking IDs.

The venue was smaller than our bedroom. The whole place was painted black, and the only lights were a single lightbulb over the bar and a small spotlight pointed at the stage area. Jeff introduced me to the band. Their instruments looked handmade. One guy had a contraption that was made of doorknobs and elastic bands, another was clutching a sheet of metal that was going to be played with something that looked like a hairbrush, and there was a woman holding a modified wooden coatrack that I was sure I'd seen at IKEA. And there was a bass player. After introductions, we stood at the side of the room. The place was tiny, but it never completely filled up. Somehow, I wasn't surprised.

The band started playing, and it was... well, noise. The bass player was hitting random notes that seemed to respond to the other sounds the strange instruments were making. Every "song" sounded alike to me. The audience was enthusiastic. I didn't get it.

Jeff looked at me and smiled. I'm sure he was reacting to the look on my face. He looked back at the band and then started nodding his head in a rhythm that clearly wasn't there. I gave him a puzzled look, and, throwing me a side glance, he raised his eyebrows, smiled, and started to tap one of his feet. That did it; I started to giggle.

"What on earth was that?" I said when we were back on the street.

"Noise," he said.

"I could hear that. Why do you like that stuff?"

"I find it interesting."

The guy didn't like hip hop, but he'd listen to noise.

"Jeez. Even experimental jazz would be better."

Jeff laughed. "Ok. Now that you've heard it once, you don't have to hear it ever again."

"Thank you. I'm going to hold you to that."

The noise concert was horrible, but most days I would gladly suffer through another one than spend another minute with Floyd. Since I couldn't keep hiding in the music room every time he came to the door, I started letting him in the house again. He'd been pressuring me to have another assessment. I couldn't bear to pay money to pour my guts out into his little magic machine, but maybe if I agreed to make an appointment, he would bother me less at home. And I had to keep reminding myself: I was doing this for Jeff.

So, I caved. I agreed to have another assessment. Both Jeff and Floyd were pleased with this decision. I, however, was miserable.

I had never been to the center without an escort before. Just walking in the door made me uneasy. It felt like I was joining them, that I was becoming one of them, that I might never come out the same. Floyd was waiting for me near the greeters' desk, and we went up to the room together. I grabbed onto the psych device, and when Floyd told me to, I closed my eyes. I tried to think of something to talk about. Then I thought of Breezie, and the psych device responded.

"Okay. I have one."

I told Floyd about her not telling me about the meeting and then asking to get her coffee. Apparently, I was still riled up about that because the machine was making all kinds of sounds. Floyd had me repeat the story a few times, and then he wanted me to think of another, analogous story. I didn't know what to say, so I thought I'd talk about the day I met Jeff's ex, Helen.

I met her early on in our relationship, a day when Jeff and I were out record hunting. We were in the mall, and we heard someone calling his name. We stopped, and she came running up to us. There was a Christie-Brinkley look about her, and she had one of those toothy smiles that made her look surprised. She was wearing expensive, sexy clothes and intricately painted-on makeup and nail polish. I was wearing my record-hunting clothes: jeans and a t-shirt. I looked at her and turned into a toadstool.

"Helen. Good to see you." Jeff put his arm around me and squeezed. "This is Melody."

"Hi," she said and dismissed me. "Jeff, your mother tells me you're looking for a new job."

"Yeah. I'm trying to find something full time. Something a little more stable."

"Well, that's wonderful." She had a sickening tone of condescension, and she kept touching him. I tried not to hate her. "Well I know you'll land a good job. You were always so smart."

He laughed. "If I were smart, I'd be living in the City."

"Why would you want to live there? It's dirty, and people are so rude."

Jeff and I exchanged glances. Apparently, Helen was a delicate flower, who, if transplanted out of her pot, would be crushed under the weight of the evil New York City.

"Marie and I had a nice time the other day," she continued. "We made cookies, and reminisced. Remember that last Christmas our two families spent together?"

"Yes. That was... uh... something."

"Wasn't it? We were singing Christmas carols around the dining room table...."

"...each in his own key...." They said this together.

It was very cloying. I tried not to show my disgust. The three of us stood in silence for a few moments, and I couldn't help thinking about how tall they were.

She finally said, "Well, we must get together. It's been too long. And Buster misses you."

"Well, give Buster a hug for me," Jeff said. I noticed he made no effort to set an actual date. She gave him a long hug, and then turned to me and said, "Well, nice to meet you, Melanie."

I didn't correct her. I didn't plan on ever seeing her again.

This story seemed to please Floyd. I could hear it in his voice. After the usual repetition of the event, he told me to think of something pleasant. I chose seeing our white rabbit. I still thought these assessments were pointless, but at least I got through it. And, although it was hard to tell with Floyd, he did seem satisfied.

Jeff, meanwhile, found a job in a record store, a real bona fide, vinyl record store, with racks and racks of old, rare, and new LPs, CDs, even singles. Cutler's was well known among audiophiles. They sold some very high-end turntables and other audio equipment, which I assumed was what had kept the store in business all this time. Jeff had been a local celebrity for years, and he certainly knew a lot about music. They were thrilled to have him. And me, I was happy he found something to do with himself besides having his brain washed clean by Floyd.

It was a Saturday morning. Jeff was about to leave for his first day of work, when the doorbell rang.

This was early for Floyd. Jeff let him in. Instead of sitting and making himself at home, he stood by the door.

"I know you two have things to do this morning. I'll be brief. I understand that I may be pushing the both of you too hard at this point. New perspective into the teachings is what is needed now. I am going to assign new assessors to each of you. They will be in touch."

This was the only time anything that Floyd said made me happy. Nevertheless, I couldn't wait for him to go.

"See you tomorrow at services."

And with that, he turned and left. But make no mistake: he'd be back.

I was recounting my daily notes on the Church of Floyd to Tamara and Laura as we were setting up our project in one of the drafting rooms. Gemini had a number of these; there were no drafting tables in them, just three or four computers and a center table. The name was left over from a time when people actually drafted. By all rights, we should have called them design rooms.

"So, is Floyd gone?" Laura asked.

"Floyd will never really be gone. He's like herpes."

They laughed. I continued.

"Jeff said Floyd wants to be part of something called Tier 12. I don't know exactly what that means, but that's supposed to be a big deal. It's like being a Grand Wizard or something. Anyway, I think he's been assigned to us, and he'll do anything they tell him to do. He's not going anywhere, count on it."

Breezie walked by the room with Anton. The three of us got very quiet.

"Melody feels the same way we do," Laura whispered, although Breezie was long past our room, and couldn't care less what we thought of, well, anything.

"About...?" Tamara said, and when Laura nodded yes, she said, "That's good to know."

People tend to bond against a common enemy, and while I had always liked Laura and Tamara, we certainly got closer after we realized that we, well, had a common enemy. Tamara liked to call Breezie "Gucci," since she was such a designer clothes hound. Laura and I took to calling her that sometimes, too, as in "Heads-up; Gucci at two o'clock."

"You know, since you've joined our team, Gucci has

been leaving me alone," Laura said. "In fact, she's downright ignoring me, like she's pretending I don't exist."

"Well, she knows I have Anton's ear. Maybe she's afraid I'll rat her out."

"Would you? That doesn't sound like you."

"It's not. She doesn't know that. Evil people assume everyone acts like them."

Then, as they say, shit got real.

The next morning, I parked the car at the office. I walked to the building. And there, off the path, standing near the last car in the lot, was a guy with an ugly, plaid jacket, like that guy from the mall. The same, ugly, plaid jacket, the knit cap, the weird glasses... that same guy.

That was really him, right? Not a doppelganger. Not a hallucination. He was standing by a white sedan, stupid giant glasses on his head, checking his phone. Wasn't he cold, dressed like that? Maybe he worked in the building. By the time I decided I was going to confront him, he had disappeared.

Someone was trying to gaslight me.

I slowly turned back around and hurried into the building.

When I got to my desk, I called Dr. Osgood. She could see me over lunch for a half hour, but I told her that Jeff couldn't know I was coming. Also, I needed to start paying her in cash.

I felt like I was in some kind of badly written spy novel.

I had to explain to Dr. Osgood why there was the need

for secrecy. This situation was getting more and more intense. I refused to let it break up Jeff and me, but here I was, doing something behind his back.

We finally got around to the reason I was there. Dr. Osgood was worried about my safety.

"Have you called the police? You could report him as a stalker."

"No. He's just a guy with an ugly, plaid jacket and a third-party smart phone. I figure he's a Church guy. Floyd must have sent him to keep an eye on me."

"A plaid jacket?" she said, seemingly concerned.

"I'm not even sure he's following me. But I guess it's a very odd coincidence if he's not."

"That's not a coincidence. He's following you."

I was surprised she was so adamant. "Well, okay, but I can't call the police. I don't want Jeff to know about this. He'd get so worried. I should be able to avoid this guy. That jacket is easy to spot."

"Okay. But keep your distance."

Anton made me the lead designer on a new, smaller project, and I requested Laura and Tamara to work on my team. Tamara could sketch anything. She went to the Fashion Institute of Technology (FIT) in the City, double-majored in Interior Design and Fine Arts. In fact, I believed she still did some painting in her spare time. And Laura, well, she was talented, and someone had to protect her from the harpy.

Last year's collection was going to be displayed at the upcoming 10th Anniversary event. Our showroom would be open to the public, they would serve appetizers and drinks, and there would be a DJ playing electronic music. I didn't have many pieces in the show, but Anton asked me to be there, so I felt I had to go. Laura, Tamara, and their husbands were going, so I'd have people to talk to. I assumed Jeff wouldn't join me.

"I'd love to go."

This weird Jeff clone was full of surprises. "Really? You usually hate these things."

"If you have to go, I'll go with you."

I went out and bought a new outfit. The female designers really dressed at these events. The men could get away with wearing just about anything. I wouldn't be surprised if they let Jeff in wearing his robe. He did rise to the occasion somewhat. He put on a sport jacket with his dark blue shirt and jeans. I was wearing a black dress with sequin accents and new stiletto heels I had to practice walking in. I chose a different necklace; it killed me not to wear my yin-yang symbol, but it wasn't very dressy.

The showroom was decorated with black, purple, and gold balloons and streamers. It reminded me of a New Year's Eve party. Tiny Laura, in a pale blue stretchy dress that accentuated her dark brown hair, and her husband, Roger, in a steel gray dress shirt and black jeans, were already there, and already drinking.

After introductions, I whispered to Laura, "Is the succubus here yet?"

"Yeah. She's already latched onto Anton."

"I'd like to avoid her if at all possible, but I think we need to make our presence known to Anton."

"Good idea."

We collected our husbands and crossed the room to

find the royal party: Anton and his partner, the three chief designers from Maplewood, and Breezie, who, in a spectacular, sparkling silver dress, looked like she had just walked off a runway.

"Melody! You're here!" Anton said.

After Laura and I introduced our husbands, Breezie turned to me and said, "Well, your husband *looks* normal."

Not sure if the expressions of horror that flashed across people's faces were because what she said was awful, or simply because they felt uncomfortable. It didn't seem to bother Jeff. He just put his arm around my waist and gave me a hug.

I smiled at her, and said, "Well, you look normal, too." Then I said to the group, "I want to show Jeff around. I'm sure we'll run into all of you later."

We turned around and saw a man pointing a camera at us. I had forgotten they hired photographers for these events.

"Wait, everybody. Smile at the camera."

We had to push our way through the crowd, but once we made it past the drinks table and over to the furniture, there was more room. Tamara and her husband, Dave, were sitting on one of the display couches, and we joined them.

A couple of pieces of mine were on display, but everything else, I hadn't seen before. I always tried to develop furniture that I'd like to have in my own house, not that I could ever afford my own work, but it was inspiring to think that way. Some of the other designers were much more outrageous. Our "token" male designer, Rod, had designed a couch that looked like a pile of large, fuzzy grapes. That was a hot seller, but I didn't know why.

Besides the photographers, there were beautiful, tall people dressed in black, serving champagne and hors d'oeuvres. We each grabbed a flute of champagne, and as I took a sip, there he was, across the room: my stalker, complete with plaid jacket, knit cap, and those bizarre glasses.

If this guy was trying to be inconspicuous, he was doing a bad job.

I was surprised they let him in. They did allow men in wearing just about anything, but come on. The guy saw me looking at him and disappeared into the crowd.

One thing I was starting to notice, along with that unnatural smile Jeff had some days, he was now starting to get that stare, what I had begun to think of as Floyd Face. He'd snap out of it when we talked, but it was unsettling. Creepy. Alarming.

If I thought that Jeff would come to his senses by himself, I was dead wrong. Floyd was now encouraging him to become an assessor. Also, there was some other thing—something called Tier Training, whatever that was— that he was doing, besides the assessor job. I really didn't want to be married to a Floyd clone, but what could I do? I wanted to say no, but Jeff and I never had that kind of relationship, where one of us would tell the other what to do or what not to do. I told Jeff I was worried he was taking on too much, but he told me he'd be okay, and that was that.

Sure. Floyd could tell Jeff what to do, but I couldn't. No, I wasn't bitter. I did tell Jeff he better not ever try to assess me. He agreed.

It had been a point of contention between Floyd and me that I didn't want to learn how to be an assessor and had no interest in any other training. That obviously added to his mistrust of my objectives, but I didn't care. I wasn't going to write down people's innermost thoughts and analyze their personalities, or whatever they did with that information. That was why normal people had therapists. And, hello, I'd have to pay to learn how to do it. I didn't have time to work for them to get free training, like Jeff did; one of us had to have a paying job. Eventually, my stubbornness wore Floyd down. Then he started coming by the house all the time again. That plan kind of backfired, didn't it?

We were having a rare Floyd-free evening. I made steaks and mashed potatoes, and after dinner, Jeff cleaned the dishes. I was going to go into my office to do some work, but Jeff stopped me.

"Let's go upstairs."

Really? I had to admit, Jeff was much more interested in sex since he joined the Church. I cynically wondered if they were feeding him oysters, but my attitude changed pretty quickly once we got up to our bedroom.

"You're beautiful," he said.

He pulled off his t-shirt, let it fall to the floor, and approached me. He leaned against me, and just stood there for a moment. The proximity, his velvety skin, his perfect chest, it was all making me feverish. He stood there just long enough to finish undressing, then started kissing my neck, something he knew made me absolutely inflamed. He got behind me, put his hands on my breasts, and gently squeezed and rubbed. I felt him get aroused, so I gently pushed back against him and swayed back and forth. He wrapped one leg around me and held me tighter.

The doorbell rang. I tensed up. Floyd was late this evening.

"Ignore it," he said. He lifted off my shirt, and I took off my bra. The doorbell rang again.

"Seriously. Ignore it."

I took off the rest of my clothes, and we made our way to the bed. I decided this was time to do something for him, and I started kissing his chest, his torso, all the way down, and put my mouth around him. He caught his breath. Soon he tapped my hand, and I stopped and got on top of him. I guided him inside me. His bright green eyes were wide open and glistening. When we finished, I flopped onto the bed next to him. There was no talking, just panting and smiling.

Of course, the next day, we'd have to deal with Floyd. He had the worst timing of anyone I had ever known. Or, he just instinctively knew when it was the worst time to show up and, therefore, did so.

But this time, he left a note: "Jeff and Melody — I must see you. — Floyd."

Even his handwriting was robotic. It looked like the font Serpentine.

I wondered what was so important that he had to leave a note. I got worried. He had that guy following me around. Did he know I was still seeing Dr. Osgood? Was he going to tell Jeff? What would Jeff say? What would he do?

"Will you be home at your regular time tonight?" Jeff said.

"I should be."

"Is it okay if I tell Floyd to come over?"

That was never okay, but I said, "Yes."

I couldn't concentrate at work. I was dreading this meeting. I had been lying to Jeff, and it looked like Floyd had found out. What was I going to do? Deny it? I kept trying out different responses in my head:

"You're mistaken."

"I only saw her that one time."

"Yes, I saw her, but how would you know that?"

None of these responses seemed like they would get me out of trouble.

When Floyd arrived, Jeff and I were in the music room, listening to a new band he had discovered called the Fallen Angels. They were an alternative rock band, and they were good. Very promising for a first album.

Floyd came in and sat down without us inviting him to do so.

"I'll be brief. I just came over to say that we are very pleased with the advancements the two of you are making. As you know, the Church is very concerned with keeping the family unit together. We are especially pleased that the two of you are having relations again."

Okay...what?

Was Floyd watching our bedroom now? I glanced at Jeff. He looked unnerved.

"But we do have a concern that Melody is not keeping up with her assessments schedule. These are very important, as you know."

Neither of us spoke.

"Well, that's all," Floyd said. "I'll show myself out."

When he was gone, I said, "How does he know...I mean, what the hell?"

Jeff shook his head. "I have no clue."

I woke up. I had no idea what time it was, but it was late. Moonlight was filling the room, illuminating the empty side of the bed next to me.

Where was Jeff?

Bathroom?

No, the light was off.

I sat up, pulled on my robe, and headed downstairs. He was sitting in the window, the moonglow shining on his face. I went to the window and sat with him. He said nothing for a bit, just kept looking out of the window. Then he said, "What do you think of Floyd?"

He still wasn't looking at me, which made it easier for me to be honest. I just wasn't sure which kind of honest I wanted to be.

"I'm not sure what to think of Floyd," I said.

He kept staring.

"You know? I'm not sure either."

We didn't say anything else. We sat there for a while, until we both grew tired and went back upstairs.

6

The 10th Year Anniversary event was a success, and Gemini made it into the spring trade magazines. There were several pictures of Breezie—with Anton and his partner, with each of the Maplewood designers, and one with the whole group. She had that same phony smile on her face in every shot. There was also that picture of me, Laura, and our husbands, smiling for all we were worth. And standing behind us, unintentionally photobombing the picture? The plaid-jacket guy.

These days, Jeff was becoming sad. Not I-can't-get-out-of-bed depressed like he had been, but he no longer had that bizarre smile on his face all of the time. He was more Jeff-like, and although I didn't want him to be sad, I preferred this to that alien grin. He would be fine when he left the house, but some days when he got home, he'd just anchor himself to the picture window. I'd sit with him, and he wouldn't say much, would just look at me and try to smile. Dr. Osgood was right; Philomathics was just Jeff's Band-Aid.

I was running alone one Saturday morning. Laura was visiting her in-laws, and Jeff had gone to work. Spring was well on its way; buds on the trees were peeking their heads out to see if the coast was clear. I ran by children who were attempting to do cartwheels on the lawn. I always thought that looked like fun, but even as a kid, I could never do them. I liked my feet firmly planted on the ground, not flying up over my head.

I ran around the park the long way, and I went around the pond twice. When I decided to head out of the park, I ran down the thicket-lined path toward the exit. There, up ahead, sitting on my favorite bench, was my stalker.

I stopped in my tracks. Now what?

Okay. I wasn't alone. There were other people in the park, so if he intended on murdering me, there'd be witnesses. And I had my phone. Dr. Osgood wasn't picking up—she was probably with a patient— so I called Laura.

"I'm sorry to bother you," I said.

"What's wrong?"

"I'm alone in the park. My therapist isn't answering her phone. And there's a guy from the Church waiting for me on the bench."

"Are you sure he's from the Church?"

"Pretty sure. He always wears the same ugly, plaid jacket. He's been spying on me since Christmas."

I was backing up, trying to get away and still keep my eye on him.

"Okay. I'll stay on the phone. How close is he?"

"Close enough, but I'm not sure he's spotted me yet."

"Can you call the police?"

"And say what? There's a guy sitting on my bench?"

"Ah. Good point. Can you exit another part of the park?"

"I'm going to try. Damn it, Laura, he's on my bench. My favorite bench. He's ruining it."

"I know."

I liked that she was humoring me.

I got out of the park the long way around, and left Laura to her in-laws.

When I got home, Dr. Osgood called me back.

"Are you alright?"

"Flustered, but alright. I think if this guy wanted to hurt me, he would have done it already. He certainly has had the opportunity."

She sighed. "True. But I don't like this."

"Trust me. Neither do I."

To me, the perfect antidote to Floyd and the Peabody dogma was Beatles music. Whether it was an expression of pure joy, like "She Loves You," or something with sophisticated lyrics like "Revolution," the music always rang true. And then there were such oddities like "You Know My Name (Look Up My Number)," which I maintained was genius, although Jeff and many others would have begged to differ. I considered those guys, especially Lennon, to be truth-seekers; it seemed to me they were constantly turning things upside down to see what was underneath.

The Beatles were probably the most recorded, photographed, quoted, studied, scrutinized, and analyzed acts of their time. Which always made me wonder, when Lennon was interviewed for Rolling Stone in 1970 (aka *Lennon Remembers*), he kept complaining that he wanted to break the illusion of the Beatles, show their "real" side. Didn't he want anything that was just theirs? Their own secrets, their own personal information? The guys could barely relieve themselves without someone photographing them. What was really important to me as a fan was their collective talents. Their "real" side, that was their business.

While I was in the music room listening to Lennon's *Plastic Ono Band*, Jeff returned from the gym. I had to admit, he was looking a lot more like himself these days: healthier, heavier, physically fit. He was still taking his 50 showers a week, so his skin had that unearthly, velvety sheen, but otherwise, he was looking better.

"'Isolation'?" he said, referring to the song that was playing. "Feeling a little low today, are we? That whole album is kind of dark."

"No, I'm okay. Just haven't listened to this in a while."

"I have an idea," he said. "Let's go to that little bar where we met. They should have some music there tonight. We haven't been out anywhere in too long. What do you think?"

"I think that's a fabulous idea."

The last time we were there was a few years earlier, when they had a karaoke night, but with a live band. There was a list of songs that they passed around, most of them top 40 hits from the 80s and 90s, but a lot of them were also Billy Joel songs. This was Long Island, after all.

Carrie and Ann had gotten up to sing "Oops, I Did it Again," which delighted Jeff, but made me, not a Britney

Spears fan, want to crawl under the table. Jeff reached over to the adjoining table and said, "Could I see that list?"

"You're not going to sing, are you?"

"No, we are."

"We are?"

"How many times do you get to sing with a live band?"

"All right. But I have veto power."

"Fair enough."

He looked over the list and smiled.

"Well, that settles it."

"What?"

He pointed to a song on the list: "When I'm Dead and Gone."

"I can't believe they play that."

"They do, and we're going to sing it."

"But I don't know the lyrics."

"They give them to you."

He had an answer to all my objections. So, we got up and sang.

We had what I liked to call I-sing-with-the-radio voices. Not bad, but don't ask us to belt out "The Man That Got Away." We even had harmonies going in places. Mostly, we survived and didn't sound like braying asses.

That was then. I just hoped tonight wasn't going to be a karaoke night. While I set about finding some clothes that were sexy but would work for this bar, Jeff was in the shower. I was dressed by the time he came out of the bathroom, and he said, "You look great."

All he had on was his new robe. I said, "So do you."

He smiled. Still no laugh, but we were getting there.

It was a typical Friday night, in a typical bar on Long Island. Chunky, overly made-up women, sporting perfect hair, sexy blouses, and leggings, arrived with their t-shirt-and-jeans-clad husbands. While I felt underdressed, my t-shirt-and-jeans-clad husband fit right in. The bar was smaller than I remembered. Jeff and I found a table near the stage area. Since neither of us were really drinkers, and one of us would be driving home, we shared a beer and an order of fries.

The entertainment tonight was a band covering mostly 70s guitar-rock songs. Jeff and I were okay with that; we owned a lot of that music. It was just nice to be out. A small group of women started dancing, and, since Jeff, like the other husbands in the bar, didn't want to dance, I joined them for a couple of songs. When I returned, Jeff put his arm around me, and I was the most relaxed I'd been in months.

The second set wasn't quite over when Jeff leaned over to me and said, "I think I better go." I looked into his gray eyes.

"No problem. Let's go. Do you want me to drive?"

"Yeah. I think that would make sense."

At home, he changed into pajamas and his robe and sat in the window. I sat with him for a long time, even though he had nothing to say.

I still considered this evening to be a breakthrough.

I was supposed to have one of those stupid assessments the next day, but I was worried about Jeff and rescheduled—they wouldn't let me cancel, and, besides, I'd already paid for it. I called work for Jeff. I just said he wasn't feeling well. Unlike the Church, they didn't feel the need to know all of our business.

I sat in the window with my cup of coffee. I was starting to understand why Jeff liked sitting there. The sun hit just the right way on my face; warm but not hot, bright but not glaring. Outside, birds were landing on trees and telephone lines, and bunnies were hopping around on people's lawns. Inside the house, dark and gloomy. Through the window, opportunities.

My neighbor Jeanine was in her yard. I tried to get her attention, but she went back inside without seeing me. When I turned my head back, Mr. Plaid Jacket was looking in our picture window, right in my face. I screamed, but when I realized who it was, I got mad. I flung open the door, and he ran.

"You better run, you little creep!"

He was halfway down the block when I had a sudden urge to run after him. I started running, and when he looked back and saw me, he went into a mad dash that I couldn't possibly keep up with. I stopped and admitted defeat.

Out of breath, I walked back to the house. Jeff was coming down the bedroom stairs. I tried to breath normally.

"Were you out running?"

"Uh, just a short run around the block."

He nodded. "Look. I'm sorry about last night."

"You have nothing to be sorry about," I said. "I had a great time. And it wasn't like we walked out on Springsteen or something. Hungry?"

"Famished."

"Great. We'll have lunch together."

Was the Real Jeff, inch by inch, minute by minute,

trying to return?

Anton was giving Breezie all of the big clients. Theoretically, they would have gone to me, but with Jeff being indisposed and me trying to help him, I realistically couldn't expect too much. I realized Anton would have to replace me, but did it have to be with Breezie?

A representative from Maplewood came into the office for a meeting, but first stopped by my desk. I stood up to shake his hand.

"Hi, Todd. Good to see you."

"We've missed having you on our projects. I hope things get back to normal soon."

"Me too."

I saw Breezie staring at us as we talked, and she wasn't smiling. I liked that.

"Anton says the project you are on now is going well. I'll be looking forward to seeing it at the next company event."

Before we said goodbye, he handed me his card. Company representatives love to give out their cards. He headed for the main conference room. I made sure I looked Breezie in the eye. Hell, I had a stalker. I wasn't afraid of a gorgon.

Jeff had decided—and was encouraged by the Church— to go visit his parents. This was huge, that he would be going there alone. They were two towns over, past Elmont, in North Valley Stream. I let him take the car, so he drove me to work, and Laura said she could drive me home.

I wasn't even thinking about this until I got a call from

Jeff's mom.

"Marie. Is everything all right?"

There was a pause. "Everything was.... Do you think you can take a car over here when you leave work and pick him up?"

"Of course. Is he talking?"

"A little. We were having such a nice visit. Now he's sitting in the kitchen with me, but he hasn't been saying much."

I was used to that. At least he wasn't curled up in a fetal position on the carpet in their bedroom. "Okay. Keep talking to him, even if he doesn't answer you. I'll call you when I'm leaving."

Tamara and Laura said they'd be okay without me for the afternoon, so I stayed until we were at a good stopping point. Then I ordered a car and called Jeff's mom to tell her I was on my way.

I went outside to wait and sat on the curb. I could have waited inside, but I wasn't thinking straight. I just wanted to be there, now. I fiddled with my yin-yang necklace and tried to be calm. Jeff would be fine. I'd take him home, have him sit in the window. It would probably take a day or two, but he'd recover.

Marie called over the weekend.

"Listen, dear, can you meet me for lunch?"

"Uh, sure. Is everything all right?"

"We need to talk."

Jeff had the car, so Marie drove to Floral Park, and we went to a diner in the village center. I couldn't figure out what she could possibly want to talk about that we couldn't discuss over the phone. We were sipping our coffee, and she put hers down and said, "I've read up on some of Philomathics' tactics."

"Tactics?"

"Leaving this church is not easy. When people leave, there are these groups called the Crow Posse that come to your door in hazmat suits and threaten you."

This Church was part religion, part CIA, and part Devo.

"Why?"

"It's to keep members from defecting. Failing that, they want to make sure that no ex-members criticize the Church or tell any of its secrets. There was a case in Long Island where a young woman sued them for harassment. And one ex-Philomathist said he was spied on, held against his will, and brainwashed."

I didn't have the heart to tell her I was already being spied on. The guy wasn't very good at it, anyway.

"Brainwashed?"

"Held captive, deprived of sleep, tortured. Brainwashed."

I did know what brainwashed meant.

"I don't think Jeff and I are in that kind of danger. We're small potatoes. Besides, we haven't openly criticized the Church. They have no reason to come after us."

"Not now," she said, "but I'm hoping for a day when the two of you will cut ties with them. And then, there's reason to worry."

She let me think about that before she continued.

"I'm also worried, dear, that if you decide to pull away first, it will tear you two apart."

"But isn't the Church all about the family unit?"

"That's what they say. But if you leave the Church, for example, and Jeff stays, they could encourage him to avoid you. They call it, 'isolating.'"

If they had a term for it, there was reason to worry.

She drank from her coffee before she continued. "I wanted to warn you, but I didn't think it was wise to do it over the phone."

"Marie, I don't know what to do. Jeff and I are in this thing up to our necks. Jeff believes the Church is helping him. He's holding on strong."

"Couldn't he just have found God like other people?"

"I wish, but instead, he found Floyd."

It seemed like there were a lot of facts about the Church available online, if one dug deep enough. The scary thing was, what about the details we didn't know, the sort of things only highest-level people knew? If the more commonplace facts were this bad, what about the real secrets?

7

In the beginning, there was Jeff and Helen. They'd known each other since grade school and were fourteen when they decided they should change from friends into something else. It was a mutual decision, and no one was surprised. Their relationship lasted past college, past Jeff in broadcasting school. Then, Jeff had a realization. Not only did Helen know nothing about music, she didn't care to learn. In fact, he was starting to think that maybe she was tone-deaf. Her only ambition seemed to be becoming Mrs. Jeff Hollenback. What Jeff discovered was that he was bored and had been for a while.

Helen and Marie had known each other most of Helen's life, and were therefore very close. They were both devastated when Jeff broke it off. Helen would go to Marie's to get consolation, and Jeff would make sure to avoid the house when she was there. Of course, the woman who replaced Helen became the enemy. I think she still is. I was lucky that I arrived later on the scene.

Thinking about Helen now, I wondered how she would have dealt with the depression, the cult, the stalker, and with Floyd. Would she have been up to the challenge? Would she have joined the Church? Would she have been better at this than I was?

Jeff was spending more time in the window, gazing out at the street. Sometimes I'd turn on some music, sometimes I'd turn on the television, then I'd sit next to him. He would eventually get hungry, and I'd make him something to eat. He hadn't been this bad in some time.

After four days of this, he decided to go to the center.

"I feel guilty," he said. "They expected me to work this week."

"Are you sure you're okay?"

"I'll be fine."

We had breakfast together, and he ordered a car.

When he wasn't home by nine, I called him and got his voicemail. I didn't know what to do, and I was starting to panic. I called Dr. Osgood, then I called Marie. We decided not to call the police just yet, although I wanted to. At ten, a car pulled up, and someone rang the doorbell.

It was Floyd. I saw two men behind him helping Jeff walk; they were almost carrying him.

"Jeff needed assistance today. He became unresponsive, so we treated him."

"What did you do to him?" I was furious. Floyd looked through me.

"A special assessment process for psychological issues."

The two men in those blue steward jackets helped Jeff in and placed him on his feet. He came over and hugged me.

"He's tired, but the treatment was a success."

Jeff wouldn't stop hugging me. I looked at Floyd.

"Please get out." I said this, literally, through my teeth.

"As you wish."

And they were gone.

Jeff stood up straight and looked at me. His eyes were gray, and he was sweaty.

"I've got to take a shower."

He was talking. That was good.

"Do you want something to eat first? You must be hungry."

He didn't respond.

"Jeff?"

"Uh, yeah. Something to eat would be good."

I heated up some leftovers for him and poured a glass of juice. Then we went upstairs, and he flopped into bed without his shower.

I had murder in my heart. These people were torturing him, abusing him, taking advantage of him. Somehow, this was going to stop.

Jeff slept most of the day and woke up with green eyes. He took a shower, came down, and had an early dinner with me. When the doorbell rang, I said, "I hope you don't mind, but I don't think I can handle any company right now."

He smiled. "Me, neither."

He was feeling better.

"Should I tell Floyd to go away?" he said.

"Yes, please."

He went to answer the door. I couldn't hear what they were saying, but Jeff came back without the evil Floyd.

"He's gone," he said. "He just wanted to check on me."

He could have called. "Thank you. That really freaked me out yesterday."

"I understand. That must have been scary seeing those guys carrying me in like that."

I didn't want to push it, but I said, "It really was."

He took my hand. "I'll be all right. You'll see."

I didn't know what to think, but that was something I wanted to believe.

He went back to bed, but instead of just lying there, he was reading one of my Le Carré books. This, alone, was an improvement.

By now, I was getting used to the Philomathics Center, the odd salesmen-like people who ran the place, even the other-worldly architecture. The guy who replaced Floyd as my assessor was just as creepy as he was. The Church must have had some kind of assembly line where they manufactured these folks. Sort of like Barbie dolls: some with red hair, some with darker skin, some with glasses, but all from the same mold. He had that cyborg stare, he never smiled, and he was devoid of emotions. I suspected that that was how they trained the assessors to conduct themselves when working. Jeff was learning to be an assessor. Was he going to be acting like that?

"Today, let's talk about something you haven't explored," the assessor said. "Your parents died young. Why don't you talk about that?"

This was new. When Floyd did the assessments, he never asked me about specific memories before. What ever happened to sharing what you wanted to share? And how did he know about my parents?

"I'd rather not," I finally said.

The assessor was furiously writing something down.

"All right," he said. "What about your relationship with your brother?"

How did he even know I had a brother? And what did I say? I hadn't spoken to Drew in years.

"We don't speak that often."

"And why is that?"

Seriously, dude, let it go.

"We hardly have anything to say to each other. He's several years older, and he's a banker."

"Let's talk about that."

Wasn't my time up yet?

"It's no big thing. We used to make an effort right after my parents died, and now we don't. We just got out of the habit."

Two hours. What on earth did he expect me to say that he had to keep me for that long? When he finally let me go, I practically ran out of there. As I was heading for the exit, I heard a woman calling: "Melanie!"

Could she be talking to me? I turned around.

It was Helen. She came up to me and gave me a hug. I didn't realize we were on hugging terms.

"What are you doing here?" I said.

She was all smiles and had a pile of books under her arm. "Oh, Jeff mentioned he had joined, so I thought I'd check it out. It's really exciting!"

That wasn't the word I'd use for it. And when did Jeff talk to her? "How long have you been coming here?"

"Oh, this is only my second assessment," she said, and

flipped her gorgeous Rapunzel-like hair off her shoulder. "I have a long way to go."

"Right," I said. I was really trying to be civil, but I wasn't sure it was coming across.

"He told me you've been coming here a while. Which Tier are you on?"

"I... uh... don't do the Tier Training."

"No?" She looked dismayed for a split second, and then her smile returned. "Well, I'm sure you will when you get a chance."

"Exactly." I didn't feel the need to tell her my business. She'd probably find out from somewhere eventually, anyway, like everybody else did.

"Well, give my love to Jeff," she said. "They're waiting for me upstairs."

She waved. I waved. And I thought, "What the hell?"

That night, I settled into my home office. I had a design idea for the project I was doing with Tamara and Laura, and since Jeff wasn't home yet, I decided to work on it. Jeff didn't get home until close to 8 o'clock. They had him in Tier Training all day, and he came home tired and cranky. And the next day he had to be an assessor all day to pay for the next round of training.

"Hungry? I called for a pizza."

"Excellent. Man, I'm bushed."

Jeff came into my office. He looked over my shoulder and said, "Nice."

"What?"

"Your design. Nice."

"Thank you."

"Also, your hair. Smells nice."

"Thank you," and then, deciding I might as well mention it, I said, "By the way, I ran into Helen at the center. She said to say hello."

"She was at the center? I guess she decided to join. That's great."

No, it wasn't. "She said she had her second assessment."

"Terrific. They've been on me to recruit people, which is not really my thing. That makes two for me. That'll probably be it."

He kissed my cheek, and then went upstairs to take a shower.

I had to decide whether I should let this bother me. Jeff was here with me, not with her. Just because she was in android school, too, didn't mean I would lose him to her.

I was more likely to lose him to Floyd.

Meanwhile, this Tier and assessor training bullshit was concerning me. Jeff was coming home worn out. He was too tired to do anything but eat and sleep. Sometimes, he would just go right to bed. His health was going to suffer. This had to stop.

I wanted him to work just at the record store and give up this alien cult. I expected one day to find a large vine with pods on it in our basement, taking over the boiler and the AC and the plumbing. Whatever planet these guys were from, they were experimenting on my husband, and I didn't like it.

And exactly what I was worried about happened: Jeff didn't get out of bed the next morning.

"Are you alright?" I said.

"Yeah.... Just...you know...."

"Should I call anyone?"

He didn't respond.

"Jeff?"

"No. Just stay here with me for a while?"

I got out my phone, sat next to him, and called work. Jeff reached out and touched my thigh. As he lay there, not sleeping, I wondered what kinds of thoughts he was having. Were they sad? Did they even make sense? I held his hand. I would will him to come back to life.

He was down for a day, then spent the next day mostly in the window. I decided to broach the subject.

"Jeff... I'm worried that you're spending too much time at the center. You've been working and training too many hours. These past two days have me scared."

We were sitting in the window holding hands. Always best to say sensitive things while in body contact.

He looked at me, puzzled.

"Is that what you think caused this?"

"I'm worried that exhaustion caused this."

"But I owe them hours. I can't cut back right now."

"Not to be motherly, but you might be missing more hours by being exhausted."

He thought about that a moment.

"You might be right. I should talk to Floyd."

"Maybe you can work eight-hour days instead of 10 or 12. And maybe train a day, and assess a day, then work at the store a day. Break it up a little more."

He nodded. "Floyd said they've started me on a rapid path for growth."

Stupid Floyd.

"Maybe you can just stay on a normal path for

growth."

Jeff looked me in the eye. "Okay."

Or, give up this nonsense altogether.

I saw Dr. Osgood before going to work. These days, I only saw her in the morning or over lunch so that Jeff wouldn't get suspicious. The session put me in an inexplicably good mood. So what if Breezie was stealing our designs? So what if she was sucking up to Anton every chance she got? I decided I just wouldn't care anymore.

La-la-la. I don't care.... Okay, maybe not that good a mood.

I got to the office, and everybody was grumbling.

"Stupid Breezie."

"I hate that bitch."

"She's not even talented."

"She just steals other people's ideas."

"Why doesn't Anton see through her?"

"Because," I said, "he doesn't work with her, and none of us are telling him anything. It would make us look petty and jealous."

I started humming, and Laura approached me.

"You seem like you're in a good mood. Did something happen?"

"No. I just decided to change my attitude. Nothing is really wrong that I can't work around. I'm lucky compared to a lot of people. Maybe therapy is working."

Laura threw me a quizzical look. I smiled at her and resumed humming.

But when I got home, Jeff was in bed again.

"Jeff?"

Please be the flu, please be the flu.

"I'm sorry Melody. I'm just not feeling up to it."

Damn it. That was what I got for being in a good mood.

"Okay. Should I... call Floyd?" I hated to suggest it, but I thought that's what he'd want.

"No, uh... I'll be fine."

I was relieved. I didn't believe for a second that any of these stopgap therapy sessions, these assessments, or whatever else they did to him, were doing anything for him except making him tired. And they might be hurting him.

I sat with him in bed, holding his hand. He eventually fell asleep, and I thought he'd be alright.

However, he didn't sleep for very long. I rolled over in the middle of the night, and his side of the bed was empty. I got up, looked down the stairs, and saw he was sitting in the picture window. This went on for three days, and the third night, I decided this was worse than usual. I would call his doctor in the morning.

But we never got to that. I fell back to sleep. Soon, he woke me up and said, "Melody... What time is it?"

"Uh.... Four o'clock."

"Day or night?"

Oh god.

"Jeff? Are you alright?"

His eyes were completely dilated, and he was shaking.

"Uh, no... I think... I'm hallucinating."

Shit. I had to remain calm.

"Why do you think that?"

"The TV isn't on, but I'm seeing things on it. Also, I was sitting in the window before, and it started to snow. It's, like, May – isn't it?"

July. He was close.

"Ok. How about some vitamin B?"

My friend Carrie used to take a few vitamin B capsules to come down when she was tripping. Figured it couldn't hurt.

"Yes. Okay."

I got them for him, and as he swallowed them, I said, "I want to call an ambulance. Would you be okay with that?"

He gave me the saddest look, and said, "Yes. Please."

The hospital gave him something to stop the hallucinations, and I sat with him until he finally fell asleep.

On my way out, Floyd and a couple of those blue-jacketed Church stewards were waiting for me.

"Melody."

I was wondering how the hell they knew where to find us. I wasn't up to pretending I was happy to see them.

"Floyd."

"How is Jeff?"

Not that you really care, you evil pile of shit.

"He's sleeping. He seems better."

"We are concerned that they may have given him medication to stop the hallucinations. The Church has other ways of dealing with such things."

How did they know Jeff was hallucinating? Were they tapping my phone? I couldn't speak without yelling, so I didn't say anything.

"But we understand you didn't know what else to do. This was a miscalculation on our part. We should have given you the information you would need should such an event occur."

I glared at him.

"The hallucinations are just Jeff reaching a state he wasn't prepared for, not a medical emergency. Again, we understand why you reacted the way you did."

I was trying very hard not to choke him.

"Well," he said, "if he's sleeping, we won't bother him. Let us know as soon as they release him, and we'll do a purge to rid him of the toxins from the medication."

The hell you will, I thought, but I said, "Okay."

The good news, if there was any good news, was that the hospital wouldn't let non-family members in to see Jeff, not right away, anyway. And, despite Floyd's objections, the hospital did not consider Floyd and his friends to be "clergy." Jeff was going to be there for three weeks. I couldn't stop Floyd from visiting forever, but at least we had a short reprieve.

"A breakdown is not uncommon with untreated depression," Dr. Osgood told me over the phone. I had called her when I got home; this, she considered to be an emergency. "And it can involve hallucinations. He went voluntarily, yes?"

"Yes."

"That's good."

I supposed it was good, but he would still be away from me for almost a month.

"Was he still spending an inordinate amount of time working at the center?"

"Yes. He's been exhausted."

"An excessive amount of work or stress can trigger something like this."

The stupid Church. I felt more helpless than ever.

Every day, I would come home from the hospital and find Floyd on my steps. Clever; I couldn't avoid him if he was sitting right outside of my door.

"You and Jeff are having a crisis. I need to be here to help you get through this."

Leaving us alone would have been the best thing he could have done, in my opinion.

"Let's talk about the teachings. You will feel better."

No; I wanted to throw up. I wanted to slit his ugly throat. I wanted to...

"Nothing will make me feel better until Jeff is home," I said.

He smirked at me, and said, "You'll see."

Marie offered to come home with me one evening after we visited Jeff. She thought her presence might discourage Floyd, maybe get him to leave.

Floyd stood up as we approached the house.

"Hello, Marie. We finally meet."

"Call me Mrs. Hollenback."

"Right. Of course. Forgive me for being too familiar. Mrs. Hollenback, will you be sitting in on our session?"

"No," she said. "Melody is exhausted, poor dear. I'm going to make her some dinner and put her to bed."

I could have hugged her.

"I see," Floyd said. "Yes, this has been taxing. Well, it seems you will not be needing me tonight, Melody. We will continue with our sessions tomorrow."

It seemed Marie had had a can of Floyd-Away in her possession all this time. Who knew?

Jeff finally returned home, and the hospital told us they would wean him off the medication he was on. Floyd wasn't happy, but he didn't push it. He kept saying all would be well once Jeff was purged again. I planned to do everything in my power to keep that from happening. As far as I was concerned, there was a Devil, and it was Floyd.

One thing about my joining Jeff's gym: this chain had a branch in a neighboring town with a pool. Now that Jeff was back to his normal weight, he had perfect, sculpted muscles. His hair was back to a normal length, too. Sometimes I took a break from swimming just to look at him. He was a little embarrassed by it at first, but then he kind of liked it. I considered calling in sick, so we could go home, and I could take that bathing suit right off him, but with Breezie taking over everything in the office, and me missing so many regular work hours, I had a suspicion that things were bound to be happening that I wouldn't like.

When I got to work, Laura filled me in.

"Anton has made Breezie a design manager. She's going to be choosing who works with her and will even have say over other projects. She hasn't messed with ours, yet, but I don't know what will happen once we're finished."

"You're afraid she's going to break up the band?"

Laura laughed. "Well, yeah."

"You and Tamara are doing okay without me?"

"You're not gone that much, really," she said, "and you certainly put in a lot of time on the weekends to make up for it. Don't worry. It's working out."

While work was okay for now, it turned out that I had zero power over Floyd and his buddies at the Church. As soon as Jeff was weaned off his meds, they talked him into doing another three-week purge. He would have to take even more time off from his job. I called Cutler's. It turned out, his boss was one of the good guys.

"Don't worry, Melody. Jeff will have a job here whenever he's ready to return."

Jeff came home the first night from the purge looking like a dried-out sponge. Four hours in a stupid sauna. How was this going to help anybody? And damnit, he got his hair cut short again.

"I'm going to take a shower," he said. "Want to join me?"

We lathered each other up using my shower gel. We were neck to toes covered in suds and began to rub against each other. His body felt warm and sturdy against mine. I held him between his legs and began softly stroking him. He grinned and buried his nose in my neck. He kneeled a bit, and gently guided himself into me. We held each other tightly, me, for support, and Jeff..., well, for support.

Jeff was doing okay that morning, and I managed to get into the office at a reasonable time. Tamara and Laura had come in early, and I went directly to the drafting room to join them. Our room was situated two doors down from Anton's office, so there was very little that walked by that we didn't see. Breezie and Anton passed by the room, and Breezie looked pointedly at me and smirked.

"You should tell her...," Tamara said.

"I thought you were going to tell her."

"Oh, God. Tell me what?"

They exchanged glances. "Breezie is going to represent the studio at the Furniture Expo in the Javits Center next month."

Anton had been promising me this for years; that if they ever did the Javits Center, I would be there. Actually, any expo in the City. He promised.

"Breezie and who else?"

"Rod and Anton."

In a studio with mostly women designers, why pick the only male designer to go on this trip? And why Breezie who was, technically, the most junior of junior designers? Why not Tamara or Evelyn, who, like me, were both senior designers?

"Well, I haven't been here much these days." I clutched my yin-yang necklace and tried to be calm. "Anton and Rod, I get. But, seriously, Breezie? Anyone but Breezie. I'd pick a member of the cleaning crew before I chose Breezie."

New York City. Jeff's and my Shangri-La. Our Mecca. Our Oz. Our Wonderland. Our Pathway to Liberation. Our Nirvana. To be fair, I couldn't blame Breezie. Or Jeff's condition. I could blame Anton, though, for being clueless.

The last time Jeff and I had a date in the City was over a year ago, before he became ill. We had tickets to see Eric Clapton at Madison Square Garden. They weren't great seats, but the sound was good. In the Garden, if you were up too high, the music would get distorted. People sitting on the ground floor were carrying plastic flutes of champagne back to their seats. Must have been nice.

We didn't know of a decent restaurant near the Garden, so after the show, we took a cab to our hotel and asked the concierge to recommend something that would still be open. We chose a sushi restaurant, something we didn't get to very often on the Island.

The next morning, we took the subway to the 72nd Street entrance of Central Park so we could visit Strawberry Fields. Jeff and I walked over to the Imagine mosaic, where there was a group of people singing Beatles songs, and we sat on the grass to listen to the music.

New York was our place, and since we didn't end up living there, we loved having excuses to visit. This expo that Breezie was going to was the first of many. I'd get my chance.

I got home from the office to find Floyd sitting on our steps again. He had a stern look on his face, and he stood up as I approached.

"There's something we need to discuss."

Now what?

"Jeff has requested fewer hours at the center after his purge. Thinks doing the assessments with all the training hours may have been too much for him."

"I see."

"We have high hopes for him. He's on an accelerated path."

"Like you are?"

He actually bristled; the tufts of hair on either side of his head seemed to stand up. The man did have a feeling or two.

"Fewer hours will slow his progress. I would like you to talk to him."

"Floyd, you realize he's not well. If he feels he was doing too much, I'm not going to push him into anything."

Now he was frowning. Still staring into the great unknown, but frowning. "So, you won't talk to him."

"He's an adult," I said. I sounded a bit snippy. "And I'm worried about his well-being."

He nodded.

"Just know, you won't be interfering with his studies any further."

"That was never my intention."

"There are certain things you'd rather Jeff not know, yes?"

For a brief moment, he actually looked me in the eye, and I saw evil.

"Very well. That's all for now," he said. I watched him slither back to his car, and I felt queasy.

8

Sometimes, a friendship can take an odd turn. People fade away, others dramatically exit. Sometimes, you'll never know what happened to make a person drop out of your life. Was it something you said? Was it something you did?

Then other times, the moment is obvious. It doesn't even have to be a major incident.

Carrie, Ann and I last saw each other at Ann's wedding a couple of years back. Ann's fiancé, Noah, was a Wall Street broker, and the wedding was black-tie-preferred. This was outside of Jeff's and my comfort zone, but I was a bridesmaid, so we rose to the occasion. Jeff put on his one really nice black suit, I had my bridesmaid dress altered, and we went to the wedding.

The ceremony was uneventful, which is what you want at a wedding. No one stood up and said, "Luke, I am your father!" or "You can't marry this woman; she's underage!" Everyone was well-behaved, and even the fidgeting was kept to a minimum.

But then there was the reception.

There were over 100 people there, and, of course, there was an open bar. This didn't really matter to Jeff and me, but everyone else was taking full advantage. There was a cocktail hour before the formal dinner, which gave people a chance to warm up to each other.

Jeff and I, and Carrie and her date, Colin, were sitting at a table with the other bridesmaids and their dates. As the night went on, Carrie was getting friendlier and cozier with Jeff, making him, me, and her date extremely irritated. Colin was fuming and eventually withdrew to the bar. I trusted Jeff, so I wasn't worried, but what kind of friend continuously gropes her other friend's husband? Jeff kept politely telling her to stop, removing a hand or two from his person every few seconds. But when she put her hand on the inside of his thigh, he stood up.

"You've got to stop. Now," he said.

"What?"

"You've been pawing me all night."

"I'm just having a little fun."

"It's making everyone uncomfortable."

"Oh, nobody minds."

"I mind. Everybody minds." He turned to me and said, "Let's take a walk."

We crossed the dance floor to the gifts table so Jeff could cool off. With some effort, Carrie got to her feet, and followed us.

"You're the ones who are being rude!"

The floor had a slippery sheen to it that made it difficult to even walk on, much less dance. Maybe it was newly waxed. Maybe the North Shore Junior Hockey League was coming in to play after the reception. Carrie started to run, but she slipped and collapsed to the floor, sliding into Jeff and me. She shrieked. Colin was just coming back from the bar and saw her land. He was mad at her before but now decided he would come to her rescue.

"Carrie! Are you alright?" Chances of getting laid – restored.

"No!" she wailed. "My ankle! I think I broke my ankle! It's all his fault!" She pointed at Jeff. Colin, having drunk away all of his judgement, took a swing at him, missing him by a kilometer.

Ann's father came over to help get Carrie to her feet. Her ankle was fine; it was the rest of her that couldn't stand. Ann, shoeless but still in her full gown, came scurrying over and shouted at Carrie for ruining her wedding. Thing was, nothing was actually ruined, yet. A woman slipped and fell, and there was some yelling. But then Colin took another swing at Jeff, missed, and grazed Ann. She screamed. Noah, who had been trying to console his new bride, punched Colin square in the jaw and propelled him into the cake. Now, the wedding was ruined. Since Jeff and I were the only two sober people at this event, our tolerance for idiocy was low. We made a swift exit.

My friendship with Carrie and Ann never recovered from that stupid wedding. Jeff and Ann blamed Carrie for being drunk and disorderly, which she was. Carrie, her pride hurt, no longer wanted to have anything to do with Jeff. And I was guilty by association. We never officially parted ways; we just stopped making plans.

As for Jeff, when we first moved to Floral Park, he had organized a pick-up basketball team. He used to play basketball in college, and while he wasn't basketball tall, neither were the other guys on the team, or on any of the other teams who played in this makeshift league. It was something he really loved to do, and he played almost every weekend for years until he got depressed and dropped out. We ran into one of the guys in the grocery store.

"Hey, Jeff! Hey, man, it's been a while."

"Eddie! Good to see you. Yeah, I've been... busy." He had never given them a reason for his dropping out. I knew he didn't want to say he'd been depressed.

"Too busy to play basketball? Man, it was your team. I hope you're making a ton of money."

Thank you, Eddie, and no, he's not...

"No. I've, uh, joined Philomathics." Didn't want to say depressed, but he'd tell him about the Church.

The look on Eddie's face was part confusion, part surprise, but mostly, he looked like he had something bitter in his mouth.

"Oh... Both of you?" he said. I nodded. "How's that going?"

"Uh... pretty good," Jeff said, and quickly changed the subject. "I also got a job at Cutler's Records in Mineola. Doesn't pay a lot; it's only part time for now."

"But that must be a good gig for you."

I nodded vehemently.

"Ah, she says yes. Melody, how are you doing?"

Losing my mind, thank you. "Okay. Still working at the design studio."

Once you mention Philomathics, it's amazing how fast

people want to end the conversation.

"Well, uh, I guess I'll see you around? Give me a call when you get some time. We could really use you back on the team."

"Okay. I will."

We said goodbye and then went back to shopping. I knew Jeff wouldn't call, not for a while. He wasn't well enough to get back to playing regularly, and the reality was, the Church was taking up most of his time.

Since the center had started purging Jeff, he was coming home hungry and dehydrated. I was trying to fatten him up: buying pizza, steaks, cookies, ice cream. He was finally looking healthier. I didn't want him to go back to being skinny, but this would fatten me up, too, if I wasn't careful. He was about to start his third week, so it wouldn't be long before this was over.

I bought some massage oil at the Body Shop. Jeff's skin was peeling. He was starting to look like an onion. On Saturday, I got out my massage oil, and after Jeff took a shower, I removed his robe and had him lie on the bed. I rubbed the oil into his back, and his skin was so thirsty, it just drank it in. I used most of the bottle, and soon he was fast asleep. I covered him with the blanket and got ready for bed myself.

In the morning, I was awakened by Jeff kissing my neck.

"Well, hello," I said. "Give me a minute."

There's a practicality of being awakened with kisses: First, pee. Then, brush teeth.

I came back to bed. We started necking like two 16-year-olds. It didn't take long for him to remove my PJs. We were pressing against each other, and I lay back and let him get on top of me. He started kissing me all over: my neck, my breasts, my torso, my back, my butt, my thighs, my toes. He rubbed my legs up and down and began to kiss the inside of my legs, moving back up to the inside of my thighs.

I shivered, and he continued his way up, working his kisses up my torso, up to my waist, all over my breasts, up to my neck, back to my lips. He spread my legs open and entered me, stopping just inside. I shuddered again. He went in all the way. Not of this Earth, not of this time, not of this galaxy.

We lay entwined for a while, not wanting to move. We were breathing slowly, deeply, in sync. We had places to be, he to services, I to the office, but neither of us made any effort to stir. He was stroking my hair and rubbing against my cheek with his. Finally, he kissed my forehead and slowly rolled off to the side.

"Just, wow," he whispered.

"Yeah."

"What do you say, we don't go anywhere today?"

"I'm good with that."

"Don't answer the phone...no texts ...don't make any calls...don't contact the outside world..."

"...with the possible exception..."

".... of, maybe, ordering food."

This was going to be a perfect day.

They were all calling us. Floyd, Marie, Laura, Sam from Cutler's, Dr. Osgood, the Democrats, the ASPCA, Save the Children, the Oyster Bay Carpet Cleaners, Bank of America, the Shriners Hospital, the Floral Park Library, the Merry Maids House Cleaners, Empire Health. We didn't answer one of their calls. We figured if anyone really wanted to talk to us, they could talk to us on Monday.

We did, however, order Chinese food through Door Dash.

Jeff and I had a 24-hour vacation from the world, and Monday, it was time to come back. Jeff's stupid purging was almost done, and he called Sam to tell him when he would be returning to the store. And I went back to the office.

Laura was working in our drafting room.

"How was Sunday?" I greeted her. "Did you come into the office?"

"Yeah," she said. "I thought you were coming in, too. I called you. Everything okay?"

"Very okay. Jeff and I had some uninterrupted us time."

"Really? Nice."

"It was. Just sex and food and rock 'n roll for 24 hours."

Of course, now that it was Monday, Jeff and I had people to answer to. Marie was distraught that no one got back to her on Sunday. Dr. Osgood had been concerned, but she was happy for me.

And Floyd?

Didn't mention it.

Jeff didn't see this as a problem, but I did.

"That's very un-Floyd-like," I said. "Wasn't he even concerned you missed services?"

"No, he said services were voluntary."

Right. With Floyd, nothing was voluntary. I didn't say anything more, though.

Floyd may not have cared that we ignored him for 24 hours, but his plaid-clad lackey sure did. I was in the grocery store, and there he was, shopping for oranges. When he saw me glaring at him, he ducked behind a group of other shoppers and was gone.

This guy had the disappearing part of spying down great.

Then, when I exited the store, he was outside of the market in the parking lot, standing next to my car. As I contemplated what to do, someone approached me.

"Melody."

It was my neighbor Jeanine. I hadn't spoken to her in ages.

"Jeanine. Good to see you."

"Haven't seen you and Jeff around. How's it going?"

Jeanine dressed like a fashionable soccer mom: stylish, but with hints of rebellion. I guessed she wanted to be presentable enough for sales but still approachable. She had on a gray leather jacket, a simple sweater, and blue jeans, but was wearing full makeup, and her chunky, costume earrings jutted out from under her dark-auburn, Chrissie-Hynde haircut. On her wrist was a delicate woman's watch, and her perfect nails were charcoal gray.

I looked over her shoulder. Plaid Guy was still there.

"We've been really busy. Jeff has a new job, and my job has me working weekends." Oversimplification, but I wasn't going to delve into our problems.

"Jeff got a job? That's great! I know he was having trouble with that."

"Not as a DJ, but still, it's great for him. He's working at Cutler's. He's a kid in a candy store."

"That's terrific. You'll have to come over sometime for dinner. Soon. I'll tell Tom I saw you."

"Yes, please send my greetings. I'll talk to Jeff, and we'll make a plan."

I looked up, and my stalker was gone.

When I got home, Floyd was sitting on my steps.

"Melody. We need to talk."

Again? Do we have to? I want to take a bath.

I contemplated my options and realized I didn't have any. "Okay, Floyd. Come in."

He sat in my living room, in the window, where Jeff liked to sit. I sat on the couch.

"You haven't been keeping up with your assessment schedule. You haven't had one in over a month."

Well, that was true.

"I'm here to quiz you on the material now, to make sure you're not falling behind. Then you can make an appointment to have an assessment."

But I wanted to take a bath.

"We know how important it is to have relations with your husband, but it shouldn't hinder your, or his, advancement with the teachings."

Eew. What did Jeff tell him, anyway? Was nothing we did private? Somehow, I knew we'd pay for ignoring Floyd for a day. Rather, I'd be paying for it.

He started reading from one of E. W. Peabody's books, and I wanted to cry.

I never, not in my whole life ever, felt the need to be enlightened. I never wanted to be set free. I liked being on Earth, thank you very much. I had no intention of following any pathway to anywhere. I didn't want to levitate, or read people's minds, or move objects around with my thoughts, or whatever else it was the Philomathists were aspiring to do. However, my head was full of E. W. Peabody. I could recite him, and sometimes, I could picture his sorry, black-and-white face, staring at me from the back cover of one of his books. They didn't need to brainwash me; I was doing it to myself.

Floyd telling me to listen to Peabody's audiobooks while I ran was a stroke of sinister genius. Running had always been my way of coping, of clearing my head. But I was fighting back now. I switched my iPhone back to the Beatles. I could reel off any Philomathic credo Floyd wanted me to, so I figured, by now, it wouldn't hurt to take in some other voices. Some sanity. Some levity. The boys would make me laugh. That seemed like an anti-Peabody thing.

At work, Tamara, Laura and I were taken off our project to design the booth for the Expo. Every time Breezie passed our drafting room, which seemed like every two minutes, she would stick her head in and say, "How's it going?"

I picked up a metal ruler to throw at her, but Laura stopped me.

The booth would have a long banner across the top, two side panels, a wide back panel, and an island in the center. Laura was in charge of constructing the booth in miniature; we decided on a 1:4 ratio. We had already gotten Anton to approve the designs for the center panel and the banner, so I printed them for her to use for her model.

Anton and Breezie entered the room while Tamara and I were figuring out the island piece. Anton had some ideas and was explaining them to us, but I heard Breezie say to Laura, "Kind of amateur, don't you think?"

I kept calm. "Excuse me, Anton. What did you say, Breezie?"

"I was talking to Laura."

"I know. It sounded like it was about the booth."

She smiled that counterfeit smile of hers, and said, "Oh, I was only joking with her. Nothing important."

"Oh. Okay." I gave her an equally fake smile back, and then turned back to Anton. "Sorry. Continue."

When Breezie left, Anton said to me, "I know you're disappointed that you're not going to New York. I just thought it would be hard for you to get away with your situation."

"Right. I might have had to say no." *But you didn't ask, now, did you?* I smirked at him. He wouldn't look me in the eye.

Breezie later cornered me in the ladies' room.

"It's killing you that you're not going to the Expo, isn't it, and that I am?"

She was right. It was.

"I love New York. It's no secret I wanted to go, and I should go. But Anton was looking out for me. I'll go next time."

She laughed. "You think so."

I'm not a violent person, but this woman made me want to force her head into the toilet and flush.

Jeff agreed to have dinner with our neighbors, although it took a few tries for him to feel up to going out and socializing. I told Jeanine a little bit about his condition, and she was patient.

"It's no problem," she said. "We aren't going anywhere."

We finally got there on a Sunday night. Jeff had been home most of the day and was in a bright-green mood.

"Jeff. Melody. It's been too long." Tom was wearing a long-sleeved Islanders jersey. Jeff and I were not really sports people, but, somehow, we always got along with the Giordanis.

We sat down to a dinner of stuffed shells and salad. Jeanine made a mean marinara sauce, certainly better than mine, and I grew up Italian. I had to remember to get her recipe.

"We haven't done this in a while," Tom said. "What have you guys been up to?"

Before Jeff could answer, I said, "Mostly working. Jeff has a new job over at Cutler's in Mineola."

"That's a great record store," Tom said. "Perfect for you, Jeff; although, with your collection, I guess you could be one of their suppliers. You probably have more albums than they do."

Jeff smiled his weird alien smile. Still no laugh, but I'm sure only I noticed.

"I've also been working at the Philomathics center," he

said.

Again. Nothing ends a happy conversation faster than bringing up the Church. That may be true of any church, depending on the audience, but one that believed in aliens definitely made a lot of people nervous.

Jeanine caught my eye and gave me a sympathetic look.

"Philomathics, eh?" Tom laughed. "What's that? Is that the religion with the magic underwear?"

"Those are the Mormons," I said quietly. *Please let's not discuss this.*

Jeanine read the look on my face and said, "Would anyone want more shells or salad?"

Jeff and I said yes to both, and after we were served, Jeanine changed the subject.

"So, Melody. How's the studio? Any new projects?"

This was why I loved this woman.

The rest of the evening went well. Tom had made desert, tiramisu, which was delicious. As we were leaving, Jeanine took me aside.

"Listen. You ever want to talk, you call me. I'm home most afternoons. Don't hesitate. Promise me you will."

"I will. Thank you."

As we exited, I thought I saw my plaid friend sitting across the street on the neighbor's porch. It wasn't him; it actually was my neighbor, having a smoke. I was seeing things.

It was unfortunate, and pride killing, but the Expo days went incredibly well.

"We made a lot of new contacts and potential sales," Anton announced. "Breezie was a star. Everybody loved her."

That's because they don't have to work with her.

Breezie came up behind me and said in my ear, "Looks like you won't ever be going to New York after all. Not while I'm here."

Yes, but if you fall down an elevator shaft, no one will come looking for you.

Evil, insufferable, despicable, contemptible, sinister. Or, what Floyd and the Church would call a "Contrary Person." I liked my descriptions better.

In other news, Breezie decided on her new design team: Laura and me. Oh, joy.

"First, we need to talk about your work."

I was so tired of people "needing to talk." Just say it, whatever it is.

"I've looked over the work you were doing with Tamara. It seems rather pedestrian. You'll need to shore up your game while working with me."

Pedestrian? That little charlatan who was stealing everybody's ideas was calling our work pedestrian?

"Oh? What do you suggest?" I said, playing along. Why did I tell Anton I could work with anybody?

"I think we should do something more in line with Rod's work."

Great. Fuzzy purple couches and lime green kitchen tables. I couldn't have been more pleased. If she wanted something more in line with Rod's work, why didn't she ask to work with Rod?

Because she liked to torture me and Laura.

Floyd, meanwhile, had been spending every one of our

sessions with a few minutes of, "Your Pathway to Liberation is at a very slow pace. If you would just start Tier Training, I wouldn't have to come here." Since I was never going to do that, it was time to appease him by having another assessment. I was way overdue. I decided I would vent about Breezie. The assessor took down everything I said about wanting to send her to the North Pole, poison her food, blow up her car, but he stopped me and told me I wasn't taking this seriously. For all they knew about me, that was how little they knew about me.

On my way out, I ran into Helen again. She greeted me like we were best friends.

"Melanie!"

"Helen.... How's it going?"

"I've started the Tier Training. It's so much fun! Have you tried it yet?"

"Uh... No. I'm sticking to assessments."

"Oh, you should try it! It's so great. I feel myself moving further up the Pathway at every session!"

"Well, that gives me something to think about."

"Yes! You'll love it!" There were three blue-jacket people waiting a few yards away. Helen turned to look at them, then turned back to me. "Anyway, fabulous to see you. Gotta run. Tell Jeff I said hello!"

It was like I was hit by a sudden gale-force wind. How could one person be so happy? It was unnatural.

I got home and Jeff was cooking.

"This is so nice. What possessed you?"

"You had a bad day at work. I thought I'd do something for you."

Okay, who told him that? I had to get over the idea that anything that happened to me was mine to share.

"Well, that's great," I said. "I'm going to get out of my work clothes, and I'll be right down."

Jeff had roasted a chicken and made stuffing. We both liked the legs and thighs, so we started there. He was looking me in the eye. I slowly chewed on my chicken leg and sucked on the end of the bone. He smiled, a Real Jeff smile, and did the same to his. I took apart the thigh with my hands and took each piece and slowly put it in my mouth. He pulled off a chunk and fed me. His stockinged feet were rubbing against mine.

"Want to go upstairs?" I said.

He reached for my hand and led me, not upstairs, but to the living room. We knelt down on the carpet and started kissing. We took off each other's tee shirts, and he unhooked my bra and softly sucked on my breasts. I unzipped his jeans and was reaching into his briefs when the doorbell rang.

Floydus interruptus.

"Crap," I said.

We were in the living room, so he could see us if he looked in. Jeff helped me to standing and led me into my office.

"Shh," he said.

I pulled his jeans and briefs down and fondled him. He went back to kissing me. The doorbell rang again.

Jeff smiled. "Oh, Floyd. C'mon, we're busy."

I laughed and put my hands around his butt and pulled him to me. His butt muscles clenched under my touch.

He lifted me up and lowered me onto him. My legs were wrapped around him, partially to keep from falling to the floor. He propped me up against the wall for better leverage. I looked up and saw Floyd's face at the side window.

I stifled my scream.

I didn't want Jeff to stop doing what he was doing, and certainly, if he knew what I just saw, he would have. I quickly averted my eyes and buried my head in Jeff's chest.

"Don't stop," I muttered.

"Why would I stop?"

If it were up to me, that would be the last time we ever made love downstairs. It would take me days to get Floyd's ridiculous expression out of my head. Eew, eew, eww. Now I needed a purge.

The next morning, there were buckets of cold rain coming down, so I went to the gym to run. I was desperate to get Floyd out of my head. Talk about assessments. I needed to get this horrible memory "replaced." I had put a new selection of music on my iPhone, but, somehow, I just wanted to listen to the Beatles. Who knew how much Floyd had seen? And then, a more unsettling thought: Who knew how often this had happened?

9

I called Dr. Osgood from my car and made an appointment to see her before work.

She was suitably shocked.

"He was watching you?"

"I don't know. I averted my eyes. It really creeped me out."

"Well, that's disturbing on many levels."

"Yes. Floyd is disturbing on many levels. I want to tear off all of my skin and replace it with Naugahyde."

She laughed.

She let me talk about Jeff, and then Breezie. There wasn't much advice for her to give me about the office. Devious people tend to get ahead. That's kind of a rule.

The Devil always wins. Ah, now I get it.

After I finished my rant about Breezie, Dr. Osgood said, "You know, why don't you and Jeff plan a trip to New York? You know how to deal with him if his depression

OBIN D'AMATO

gets to be too much. It would be good for both of you, but especially for you."

Ok. This was why I still went to see her.

When I got in to work, Laura greeted me with, "Well, Breezie is out today. She has the flu."

"I didn't think demons could get the flu."

It was a wonderful Breezie-free day. The mood in the office was almost celebratory. Anton asked Tamara to work with Laura and me in Breezie's absence. Anton usually made the right call when something wasn't sucking on his neck.

Per Breezie's instructions, we were working on a living room with very bright colors. I decided to set it with a 60s feel. Tamara changed some of the weird colors Breezie had suggested, and the rich hues she used instead made everything look more current.

"This is probably the last time Gucci ever gets sick," Tamara said.

Anton liked what we were doing.

"Interesting," Anton said. "This is a departure for you."

"Breezie wanted us to use bright colors, so I thought I'd try a mid-century modern approach," I said. "Tamara changed her colors to jewel tones, and we ran with it."

I believed in giving credit where credit was due. Even to Breezie.

"Nice. It looks like you are making it work."

"Not usually my style. You know I prefer muted tones and grays, more neutral colors, with the occasional pop, not the whole exploded clown thing. But Tamara toned everything down, and now I like it."

The five days when Breezie was out proved to be productive for all of the design teams. We were thankful that she couldn't be everywhere at once, despite her Lucifer-like qualities.

Laura came in early on Monday, and when I joined her in the drafting room, I found that Breezie was standing over her. She had made changes to everything Laura and I worked on the previous week. The sketches looked like some child scribbled all over them with a red crayon.

"What was wrong with what we had?" I said.

"It wasn't good," Breezie said.

She was standing by the window. We were only on the fourth floor. If I pushed her out of the window, it might not kill her, but surely it would hurt her, right?

"Interesting," I said. "Because Anton saw the sketches and mood board on Friday and approved them."

"Well, Anton will like this even better." She walked towards the door and said, "Make the changes."

When she was gone, I said to Laura, "We have copies of these drawings, don't we?"

"Yeah, I made copies before we showed them to Anton."

"Good. I think I have to talk to him."

I helped Laura start to resketch the designs from Breezie's changes, but I suggested we not render them just yet. When I saw Anton on his way to his office, I went out into the hall, said, "Anton. Can I ask you something?"

He came in and saw the red scrawl all over our sketches.

"What's that?"

"Breezie had some changes."

"Can I see?"

He wasn't smiling, but I couldn't tell if that was good for us or not.

"I think these are unnecessary. Do you have a copy of these without Breezie's markup?"

"Sure."

"Ok. Let's go with those." He was about to leave, when he turned to me and said, "Melody, you said you had a question?"

"Yes. You answered it."

"I did? Okay. Good." He went out into the hall. "Breezie?"

Her smile disappeared as she approached the room.

"I looked over your changes. I think we'll be going with the original sketches here. I think it's more in line with what the client wants."

Will. Not. Let. The. Devil. Win.

With this victory, albeit small, I was in a much better mood. Breezie steered clear of Laura and me the rest of the day. Instead, she went around sucking the blood of other victims. This was unfortunate for them, but Laura and I had already given our share.

As I was waiting for the elevator to go home, Breezie sidled up to me. Honestly. Why couldn't people who hated me leave me alone?

"You don't like me very much, do you?" she said, with a smug smile that I wanted to punch right off her face.

No one likes you very much.

"What makes you say that?"

"Oh, just a feeling, I guess."

Get real, Breezie. Sociopaths don't have feelings.

The doors opened and she got on the elevator with me.

"Just so you know, Anton said you and Laura will be working with me for the foreseeable future."

Oh, joy.

Jeff and I planned our trip for the last weekend of the month. I didn't tell anyone at work where we were going. I was embarrassed. I didn't want Anton or Breezie, or anyone else, to know how much going to New York meant to me. I said we were going to the Poconos to one of those cheesy couples' resorts for a long weekend. They didn't need any more details than that, nor would they want any.

We took a late train. I had convinced Jeff that it would be less crowded at 10 o'clock, and he agreed, but actually, I was hoping that we could escape without any of the Church people knowing our plans. We might have found one of them in our hotel bathtub.

The hotel room, which per night cost about as much as an assessment, was small but lavish. We undressed and dove under the plush comforter. He started kissing my neck, and I began licking his nipples, which got him instantly aroused. I went further down under the covers to pleasure him. He had his hand on my head, and I slowly licked every inch of him. There was no one to interrupt us, no one to see us, no one to disapprove of what we were doing.

The next day, we had tickets to the Statue of Liberty. (Yes, the term Pathway to Liberation sprang to mind. Damn E. W. Peabody.) It was claustrophobic, single file all the way up, but when we got to the crown, despite my having a touch of vertigo, the view was like nothing else.

They didn't allow people to go up to the torch anymore, or Jeff would have insisted we do that, too. He put his arms around me and hugged me from behind. We didn't need to say anything.

It was Halloween weekend. We had dinner in the Village, an area rich in bohemian ghosts, oozing with the memories of artists, musicians, and comics from decades gone by. We walked down MacDougal Street, past the jewelry shops, restaurants, comedy clubs, and cafes, all packed so tightly together that many businesses were actually below the street. The Village Halloween Parade had just ended, and we were surrounded by costumed revelers. There were plenty of zombies and vampires, costumes which didn't take much creativity in their concept, but rallied during fabrication. One woman was wearing an antique bridal gown and heavy, garish makeup. She was holding a severed head as a purse and was talking to herself. (We hoped that that one was actually a costume.) We saw two people wrapped together in cellophane, the woman facing front and the man facing back. There was a cluster of Minions, various comic-book heroes, and a multitude of scantily clad women, most in those cheap store-bought "sexy" Halloween costumes that were two sizes too small and in danger of ripping apart. We made it to Washington Square, feeling completely invisible amid the outfitted masses that were swarming around us. Near the fountain, musicians were playing and people were singing. Stray, unaccompanied children ran around, dogs were barking, and vice versa. We cut through to Fifth Avenue and walked north. I looked up and saw a shooting star just brushing by the Empire State Building. I made a wish, but revealing it would jinx its fulfillment.

In the morning, I decided to go swimming in the hotel pool. Jeff said he'd order us breakfast. When I got back, room service had come, but Jeff was in bed.

"Jeff?"

I expected him to say, "I'm sorry Melody. I'm just not feeling up to it," but he said, "I think maybe I did too much."

"Okay," I said. We had one day left. "We don't have to leave this room today, if you don't want to."

"Are you sure? You can go do something."

"No. I want to stay with you."

We ate our blueberry pancakes, drank our coffee, and then spent the day binge-watching the NCIS marathon.

I was able to get Jeff to the train in the morning and got him home and into bed. At least he was responsive, and it seemed like he was actually going to fall asleep. I wanted to call Dr. Osgood but realized this wasn't an emergency. Instead, I called Jeanine.

"Are you busy?"

"No," she said. "I'll be right over."

I remembered that Jeanine preferred tea, so I made some. I didn't have much else to offer her, but I put out some crackers, and we sat in the kitchen.

"How long has he been like this?" She took a cracker. My hospitality, albeit pathetic, appeared to be adequate.

"Wow. About a year, I guess."

"Is he on meds?"

I shook my head. "They're up in the bathroom cabinet. He thinks the answer is Philomathics, but then he still gets like this."

"Excuse me for saying so, but Philomathics isn't the answer to anything," she said. "He needs a doctor."

"He has one, but the Church is opposed to doctors and therapists."

"And how are you with Philomathics?" she said. "You must have been learning something about it since he signed on."

"I have. It's kind of being forced on me."

We paused and sipped our tea. She said, "What are you going to do?"

"I don't know. I just want him to get better."

"Let's just hope they aren't making him worse."

"I hope that all of the time."

The next morning, Jeanine called and said, "Melody. Do you know anything about the guy who's on my porch?"

I looked out. Plaid Guy was looking in the Giordanis' front window.

I sighed. "Yeah, he's from the Church."

"What should I do?"

"He's harmless. Open the door and he'll run."

"Why is he looking in my window?"

"He's spying on you."

"That's what I thought."

She opened the door, and he ran. She waved to me and closed her door.

"So, talking to you is not allowed?"

I sighed. "Apparently not."

"Well, screw that."

I laughed.

"Have you called the police on this guy?" Jeanine said.

"No. That would start an investigation, and I'd have to tell Jeff."

"So? I think he could handle it."

"Maybe. On the other hand, he's back in bed, for I don't

know how long. I just don't think the time is right."

Jeff was back up a day later and headed in to work. Floyd hadn't been by in a while, but there he was, as soon as I got home, waiting for me.

"Shall we get started?"

At this point, I wasn't sure what I was hating more; Floyd grilling me about E. W. Peabody or paying some clown to assess me. Money, Floyd. Rock, hard place.

There was one E. W. Peabody book I was avoiding called *Philomathics: Tier Training Demystified*. I was determined not to learn anything about Tier Training. It was my only act of defiance left, my way of not becoming a full-fledged Philomathist. I think there was still a book or two that I hadn't cracked, so it was possible Floyd didn't notice I was skipping that one. Maybe it didn't matter, since I wasn't doing the training. So far, he hadn't mentioned it.

After Floyd left, Jeff and I sat down to a lasagna I had put together the other day. He looked at me with those gorgeous, green eyes, and said, "Why don't you like assessments?"

Damn. Was it that obvious? All of this time I was thinking I was being skillfully reticent, and in actuality, I had a glass head.

"We can't afford them, Jeff. If I went to as many as you did, we'd be living in a cardboard box."

"Are you sure that's all it is?"

I was so tired of lying to him. I could have said they made me nervous, which was true. I could have said I didn't like the way everything I said was written down, which was also true. But what I said was, "Yes. I'm sure."

"Okay."

I don't think either of us were satisfied with my answer.

I had the day off for Veteran's day, so Jeff stayed home, too. After breakfast, we went to the gym. I was running on the treadmill and listening to Springsteen on my iPhone, and I realized Jeff and I hadn't even tried to see him in over two years. Things were definitely bad when Jeff wasn't psyched to see Springsteen. Floyd thought music, especially popular music, was an anti-Peabody distraction. It was good for him that he hadn't shared that opinion with Jeff.

We saw our rabbit again on our way home. His reddish-brown fur was turning white. He looked like it had snowed on him. He was also a lot bigger now, and his large feet were covered in long fur. Seeing him made me happy, and I took this as a sign of better things to come.

After we had lunch, we decided to spend some time in the music room. This was going to be 80s day. It was a good decade for music. There were a lot of independent labels, and a new group was forming every other day. Jeff put on a couple of his mix CDs and set them to shuffle. He had included a lot of obscure songs, and as each one played, he'd give me the history of the band, the players, how well the record did, whatever he could come up with. A song from the Bush Tetras, "Too Many Creeps," started to play. It was a favorite of mine and so appropriate to my current situation.

It was a good day. No one was looking in our windows. No one was quizzing me. No one was annoying me. Just music and Jeff.

Friday, when I got home, I started considering my work options. Look for a new job, one that wouldn't mind me taking time off for Jeff. That would probably mean a considerable cut in pay. With the pressure coming from Floyd and Jeff that I do more assessments, we couldn't realistically afford that.

I put the soundtrack from the recent *A Star is Born* on the stereo and tried to think about pleasant things.

I could freelance. I was freelancing when I met Jeff. Maybe, down the road, I could start my own business. Maybe I could even hire Tamara and Laura away from Gemini.

Freelancing. That was a plan I could start to implement.

Jeff had spent the day at the center and came home looking weary. I took his coat from him.

"Hard day?"

"Assessments are hard work," he said. "I'm not supposed to be getting emotional, because that could interfere with their progress, but I can't help feeling bad for everyone. They just want enlightenment, but there's so much pain."

My Jeff was in there somewhere.

"Floyd said the more I do, the easier they would get. We'll just have to see. Anyway, I think I'm going to call Sam and tell him I can't work tomorrow. The center wants me there."

And then there was that.

After dinner, I proposed a full body massage, emphasizing the full body part. I had him sit on the edge of the bed while I undressed him, then had him lay down on his stomach. I had bought some more massage lotion from the bath store, and I rubbed it on my hands to warm it up. I started on his neck, squeezing and rubbing until I could feel the tension melting away. Then, on to his perfect shoulders. I didn't really have the strength in my hands to get through the tautness of those muscles, but that didn't matter to him; if he wanted that kind of massage, he'd have to go to a pro, and probably, a man. I worked my way down to his lower back, which flinched as I pressed on it. I skipped down to his feet, and worked my way up his calves, his thighs, then finally, on to his butt. I separated his cheeks, and continued kneading; he moaned.

I leaned over him, and whispered in his ear, "Turn over."

He was excited and started to kiss me, and I said, "I'm not done."

On his back now, I massaged around his Adam's apple and under this chin. Then, I poured more massage lotion into my hands and smoothed it over his chest. I worked a long time on his chest, kneading around his nipples, before finally circling the tips; he gasped and closed his eyes. I slowed down, made my way down to his navel, then just below, to gently pet his pubic hair. He sat up, and I eased him back down. I waited, then poured more massage lotion on his loins and rubbed it in.

"Jesus," he muttered. At least we had a proper deity. He kept trying to move, so I knelt on his thighs and continued working, slowly and carefully, up and down, underneath, and all around, until... we were done.

"Oh, God, I'm sorry," he said.

"Don't be. That's what I was aiming for."

He was breathing hard, but managed to say, "That was so great."

I planted tiny kisses all over his face and neck.

We took a shower together, and then my tall, brawny, perfect, green-eyed, Apollo dropped into bed and fell asleep. I watched him for a long while. Maybe I had purged him of Floyd and the Floydettes, just for the moment.

There was a little café in town where I liked to work sometimes. I went there the next morning, set up my laptop in a seat by the window, and proceeded to scan the classifieds. The New York Times had an abundance of design jobs, most of them book or package design, not interior design, but I went over the list and took down whatever I thought I could do. Then I found something interesting: working for IKEA. This would be a step down from the high-end stuff I was used to doing, but I loved IKEA. It really would depend on how badly I wanted to leave Gemini. The job description stated "flex hours," which might have worked even better than freelance. It was the Hicksville IKEA, which was further into the Island, just a car ride away. I filled out the online application.

"Melody?"

Marie had come over to my table. She was dressed in blue slacks, with a coordinating blouse, purse, and boots. In design lingo, they would've accused her of being too "matchy matchy," but I liked the way she pulled it off.

"A little Christmas shopping?"

She was carrying three large shopping bags. She laughed. "Yes. I went to Roosevelt Field. I got a little carried away. What are you doing here?"

"Drinking coffee. Doing some work. I felt like I needed to leave the house for a bit."

"And Jeff?"

"I dropped him off at work this morning." I took a sip of my lukewarm coffee, grimaced, and put it aside. "Sit."

She climbed onto one of the café's tall stools. This place thought that everyone was seven feet tall. When the waitress came by, Marie ordered a coffee and a blueberry muffin, and I asked for a fresh cup of coffee.

"By the way," Marie said. "I found something out about that Tier Training they keep referring to. It's apparently geared toward teaching people how to respond to certain situations."

She poured four Sweet 'n Lows into her coffee and stirred it. I forced myself not to make a face; I liked mine unsweetened, and this seemed excessive.

"The first exercise is called Acknowledging," she said. "The trainer and the trainee sit across from each other, and the trainee tries not to move or blink too much. I think they have to sit there for an hour. If he passes the test, he makes it to Tier 1."

Was that the crazy android eye thing Floyd and Jeff did? The Church claimed Tier Training was supposed to be the fast track to enlightenment. Why were people so intent on being enlightened, anyway? It seemed to me it just separated you from the rest of humanity.

I looked up, and from my seat in the window, I saw my stalker. I must have frowned, because Marie said, "What's wrong?"

I hesitated, and then decided it was time to tell her. "Well... don't tell Jeff, but there's a guy outside who has been following me for, like, a year."

Of course, she was alarmed. "Why didn't you tell me?"

"I didn't want anyone to worry. He's pretty harmless, and he's easy to spot with those stupid, ugly, plaid jackets he wears. I've almost gotten used to having him around."

She looked out of the window.

"See the guy leaning on the car, wearing the knit cap and the weird glasses?" I said. "That's the guy."

"Not very subtle..."

"No. He clearly wants to be seen."

"I'm going to have to research this fellow. Surely there's something on the internet about the Church following people around."

We turned back to our coffee.

"Have you called the police?"

"No. He hasn't gotten too close, and if I call the police, Jeff will know something is going on. I'm afraid that if I tell him the Church has sent someone to follow me around, he'll think I'm being paranoid, or worse, anti-Peabody."

After Marie and I said our goodbyes, I made a lot of headway with my applications. Just thinking about leaving made me happy. I still wasn't sure I'd actually do it.

Early Sunday, Jeff walked over to the gym. I was trying to decide whether I was going to go running or not. It was frosty, and I could have gone to the gym with Jeff, but I wasn't feeling particularly athletic that morning.

I wondered if there was even a reason for me to be

awake yet. I stretched, not unlike a cat, and looked over at the stack of books Jeff kept on his nightstand. *Philomathics and You*, *Philomathics and Your Neighbor*, *Philomathics All the Way*, and then the one I'd been avoiding, *Philomathics: Tier Training Demystified*.

I was curious. The question was.... Did I want to know?

I pulled it from the stack and opened to a random page.

"The trainee and the trainer sit facing each other and look into each other's eyes. The test ends when the trainee can sit for an hour without excessive movement or blinking."

That was that Acknowledging thing Marie had mentioned. I flipped through the book a bit further to Communicating.

"The trainee uses pantomime to communicate to the trainer a series of tasks the trainer should do. After the trainee is successful, he repeats the exercise using vocal commands."

But that sounded stupid. Clearly, I would be understanding this better if I read the book all the way through, but I jumped ahead again.

"Using vocal commands, the trainee makes a fork move across the table."

Seriously? That was ridiculous.

I reached over to put it back in the pile, and my phone rang. I picked it up from my side table. Marie sounded distressed.

"Marie. What's wrong?"

"Someone slashed our tires."

"What?!"

"Frank went out to go to the store, and he found the tires slashed. All four of them."

"Oh, no...." Wow. These were some very screwed up people.

"You don't think it's the Church," she said. "I mean, why would they...."

I sighed. "Because they saw us talking. And they're insane."

"Well, we're going to call the police. We have to fight back."

I wasn't sure that was going to help, but there was nothing worse than feeling you couldn't do anything, like I was feeling.

"Is it possible it was neighborhood kids?"

"Do you really think that?" she said. "Our neighborhood kids don't do that kind of thing. They didn't toilet paper the house. They attacked our car with boxcutters."

"True. Just trying to think of other possibilities."

She got quieter, and said, "Don't tell Jeff. We may put him in danger."

"Agreed."

Naturally, the police assumed what I had said: local kids. Sure, always blame the kids. Never consider some nut-job who belongs to a cult.

"The officer said they'd let us know if anything develops," Marie said.

I didn't want anything else to develop. I was feeling terrible about this. It wasn't my fault, but just like any other mob, if they couldn't get you to comply, they'd go after the people you love.

They already had Jeff. What more did they want?

Everything. Power. Money. World domination. I wished they would just find their spaceship to whatever planet they were from and go back home. And leave us alone.

Floyd wanted me to do something called a Reliability Assessment. I didn't know what that meant, but I had agreed to do it. He was insisting, and I was beginning to worry he might figure out that I was a fraud. I had run out of excuses, and apparently, the Church considered them mandatory after your first year. The money was worth it to maintain my deception, and it was still cheaper than the Tier training I'd been avoiding.

I didn't know what to expect. It had to be like a regular assessment, right?

The assessor started by asking me questions.

"Why did you join the Church?"

That stumped me, as I didn't feel like I had.

"Because of my husband, Jeff," I said.

"And why do you think Jeff joined the Church?"

"Uh.... He had been depressed, and he said it was helping him."

"So, has Jeff shown signs of improvement?"

"Well, yes, but—"

"And what do you attribute this improvement to?"

Oh, bite me.

"Food and sex," I said.

The assessor didn't flinch. He reminded me of those guards in London with the big furry hats.

"And how often do you two have sex?"

I walked right into that one. "None of your business."

He paused. "How often?"

"None of your business."

"I see. Do you think Jeff has sex with anyone else?"

"No. I don't."

"You seem upset. Are you sure?"

"Yes, I'm sure. I'm upset because you're annoying me."

"Well, have you had sex with anyone else?"

"Ever?"

I was sorry I said that. The psych device couldn't read sarcasm.

"Since you were married to Jeff."

"No."

He was writing all of this down. Maybe I shouldn't have been so flippant.

"What kind of sex do you have?"

"Again, none of your business."

"Do you have threesomes?"

"No."

"What do you feel about this line of questioning?"

"It's intrusive."

"Do you have any negative thoughts about Mr. Peabody?"

I jerked, practically dropping the psych device handle. The machine went crazy.

"Do you?"

I tried to calm myself down. "Uh... No. No, I don't."

I was sure the machine could tell I was lying. The assessor kept repeating the question. I tried to outsmart the machine. I tried repeating a mantra to myself that I was given when I was 14. I tried to slow down my breathing. Nothing was working. He continued interrogating me.

"So, you do have negative feelings about Mr. Peabody. What about the center? The Church?"

"No! I... I..."

Eventually, the assessor got off the anti-Peabody questioning. Even so, I felt like I had just been on trial, and asked if, yes or no, had I stopped beating my husband, and had I ever been a communist?

After that, the center started calling me.

"Melody. Your Reliability Assessment was a disappointment. It's time that you start Tier Training. Don't you want to be on the same Tier as your husband?"

Hanging up wouldn't have been an option. They'd just call back, or put a curse on me, or something.

"If I was concerned about that, I'd have started with him," I said. "I'm not interested in Tier Training. I can't afford it."

"You could work it off. We're very open to members working off their training."

"I'm already working. We only have a one-income household. I don't have time to do anything else."

That usually did it. Until the next hour or so, when someone else would call back and ask the same thing. I finally turned off the ringer on my phone. If this was all they did about me failing this assessment, I could live with that. Somehow, I doubted that was it.

I was at the market, and a woman came up to me and yelled, "Crow!" and threw something in my cart: a small bag of sunflower seeds. If I didn't know she was from the Church, I'd just think she was crazy, as did the other people who witnessed this.

"What did she throw in your cart?"

"'Sunflower seeds."

"Crazy."

"Yeah," I said. "Crazy."

Thing was, I wasn't, by their definition, a "Crow." A Crow was a defector from Philomathics who spoke ill of the organization. I was a complete, I-never-wanted-to-do-this-in-the-first-place non-believer. But having failed the Reliability Assessment, I guessed I landed on their list of Prospective Nuisances.

Out in the parking lot, a bag of sunflower seeds was on the hood of my car. This was far less disturbing than slashed tires, but they wanted to make sure I knew they were out there, watching.

Jeff was home when I got there. He said, "The strangest thing happened. When I got home, there was a huge bag of bird seed on our porch."

"I guess the birds are trying to give us a hint," I said. He smiled.

Still no laugh? I thought that one was pretty good.

Jeanine shared my passion for shoes, so she suggested we do some shopping. All of the stores were having post-Christmas sales. I let Jeff have the car, and Jeanine drove us to the Macy's in Valley Stream. We tried on everything they had, even flip-flops. There were thousands of shoes, and it was exhausting, but fun.

We took a break for lunch, then went back and chose a couple of pairs each. I was waiting in line to pay, then thought better of it. Continuously paying for assessments was stressing me out. It was throwing money in the trash and wreaking havoc with my credit. Should I really be buying myself shoes?

"What am I doing?" I said.

"You're buying shoes."

"Yes, but I probably shouldn't be. I just had a special assessment. It was expensive."

Jeanine took me out of the line.

"Listen. You're not buying Jimmy Choos. Although, they did look great on you."

I laughed.

"When's the last time you bought yourself something?"

"Uh...," I had to think. "Last month. I bought a cheesecake."

Jeanine smirked at me.

"Everything is 20% off. Buy the shoes."

We got back in line. The two pairs I picked out, combined, were less than half of what I paid for that Reliability Assessment.

We pulled into Jeanine's driveway some time later to find her impeccably trimmed hedges cut down to practically nothing. There were piles of evergreen stems everywhere.

"What the...."

We got out of the car. Jeanine was irate.

"What did they do? These bushes are hacked to death. They won't recover."

She was on the verge of tears. I felt a huge surge of guilt coming on.

"You've been spending time with me," I said.

"That's fucked up." She studied the damage, which was total, and then pulled out her phone.

"I'm calling the police. These people don't scare me."

They scared me, and it wasn't even my house.

10

Jeanine and Tom invited us to a Knicks game. They knew we didn't usually go to sporting events, but Jeanine was intent on getting us out of the house. Besides, basketball was one of the less boring sports, and Jeff used to play. At least it wasn't golf or baseball. The tickets said they were playing the Pelicans. Now who on earth were they? Considering we didn't follow the sport, they could have been playing a football team for all we knew.

The game was at the Garden, which was right at Penn Station. We got off the train, went up an escalator, climbed some stairs, and then, after maybe ten feet of walking in the January air, we were there. Fans wearing Knicks gear swarmed around us. A lot of them were very aggressive, which confused me. The seats were numbered. It wasn't like getting in faster than someone else would get them a better view. Jeanine and Tom had season tickets, and our seats were great. Probably wasted on Jeff and me, but still great.

"Okay, which ones are the Knicks?" Jeff said.

Tom laughed and pointed to his shirt. "Root for the blue and orange."

"Aha. Good to know."

Funny thing about sports. When you saw a game live, you could be the least sporty person in the place, yet you could still find yourself jumping up and down like a lunatic. Well, I was, anyway. Jeff wasn't exactly the jump-up-and-down type these days, but he and Tom were talking a lot during the game, and he seemed happy. We were rooting for the right team, so there was that. And basketball is fast and furious. Your team is down by two points, then it's up by five, then it's back down seven, then it's up four. Doesn't leave any time to get bored, and if you blink, you miss out on twenty points.

Since the game was being played right next to the train station, Jeff and I didn't really get enough of our New York time. We convinced Tom and Jeanine to take a short walk around the block so we could drink in the lights and the noise. There was a jazz trio on 8th Avenue, set up in front of the steps of the old post office. Jeff recognized every song they played and whispered to me the original artist and when the record was a hit. I could tell by the looks on Jeanine and Tom's faces that they thought he was whispering sweet nothings to me, and actually, that *was* Jeff's version of sweet nothings. On the way home, Jeff was totally relaxed; he slept on my shoulder all the way back to the Island. Sometimes, it's good to do other things than what you're used to.

I thought maybe the Church would stop harassing us if I did another regular assessment. While I hated doing assessments with Floyd, the fact was, I hated all of them. I didn't like feeling emotionally vulnerable to these bioengineered clones, but as much as I tried to avoid it, I had to tell them something. Eventually, I did talk about my parents, my brother bullying me as a kid, the day I broke up with my first boyfriend. This time, I would talk about the day my grandfather locked me out of the house in the winter. I had drawn on the wall of their living room, and in an attempt to stop my grandmother from spoiling me, he decided to discipline me himself by dragging me outside and leaving me there. Eventually, my grandmother figured it out—probably heard me shrieking and crying—and rescued me. Let's just say there wasn't a lot of talking in that house for a while. Yelling, yes, but no talking.

I still felt this was nobody's business, but I couldn't stay at the center for hours without talking, and I found the more I talked, the sooner I got out of there.

The assessor seemed pleased with my efforts. I guess he liked the grandfather story. I began to realize they tended to like stories where you sound like a victim, then after repeating the story, you realize you weren't one after all. All resolved. Next.

Late one afternoon, I was listening to Taylor Swift in the music room. It was her first album, the only one I really liked. Anyway, I was comfortably settled into one of the sofa chairs, when the doorbell rang. I looked out of the picture window and saw Jeanine, not Floyd, so I let her in.

"Hi," I said. "I wasn't expecting you. Come in. Want some tea?"

She followed me into the kitchen and sat at the table.

"You know, feeding the birds is bad for the environment," she said.

I had just fed them; they were making quite a racket.

"I guess it's good that I don't do it very often, then." I put the kettle on and looked in the cupboard for some cookies.

"And it attracts crows," she said.

I was expecting her to say it attracted squirrels. Most people had a thing about squirrels. Squirrels and blue jays.

"Is Jeff at the center?"

"No, he works at Cutler's today."

I brought the cookies to the table and sat down. Jeanine wasn't looking at me. I took a cookie and waited for her to say something.

"Anyway, I've been thinking," she said. "It's about time that you actually joined the Church."

What?

"Don't look so shocked. How long did you think you could get away with this half-assed stuff?" Her eyes glazed over into Floyd Face. "It's been long enough now. We've been waiting for you to come around. It's time."

The kettle started to boil, but I couldn't get to it because she was gripping my arm.

"Stop fighting us."

With that, I shook awake. I wasn't sure where I was, even though I could clearly see that I was in our bedroom. That dream was so real; I couldn't get it out of my head. It was the middle of the night. Jeff was fast asleep beside me, and I'm sure Jeanine was as well, next door.

Now, the Church was invading my dreams.

Even though it was icy cold, Laura and I went for a quick run the next morning. We only ran around the pond once, circled around one side of the park, then we went back to the house to change. I let her have the fancy, upstairs shower. I hadn't done laundry for a couple of weeks, and it took me a while to choose something to wear. Floyd had picked Jeff up early so I could have the car. I toasted bagels for us, and then we headed out to go to work.

But when Laura and I went outside, there was a dead animal on my hood, its blood smeared all over the windshield.

We screamed.

Tom and Jeanine rushed out of their house. We were all going to be late.

"Are you going to call the police?" Jeanine said.

I tried not to yell at Jeanine. "What for? Did anything happen when you called? No. Did anything happen when my mother-in-law called? No."

Jeanine shook her head. I was picturing Floyd's head on my car instead of that poor creature. Tom went into their garage to get some work gloves and discarded the body. Then, he came back to hose off the windshield.

"It was a rabbit," he said to me. "It was white, kinda longish fur, so at first I thought it was a possum."

No. They wouldn't.... "What?!"

"Yeah. It was probably hit by a car. Didn't want to look at it too closely, you know?"

I knew. And I was crying.

It took me a long time to calm down. Laura and the Giordanis couldn't understand why I took this so hard, and I was in no condition to explain it. The car still had residual blood in the crevices near the windshield and under the hood. I'd take it to the car wash later. Laura and I were too upset to get in the car, so we took a car service to work.

I couldn't stop thinking about it. Since I was thoroughly distracted anyway, I decided to leave early, take a car service home, and get my car washed. I offered to share my ride with Laura, but she said working helped keep her mind off of it, so she chose to stay.

The car service arrived, a huge, black SUV, which dwarfed me as I sat alone in the back seat. I wasn't paying much attention, but as I was getting out, I noticed the driver was wearing a gray knit cap, and there was a pair of what looked like goggles on the dashboard. Yes, I had an impulsive. It sounded like this: "AHHHHHHHHHHH." He sped off. Guess he didn't expect me to screech like a banshee. Frankly, neither did I.

The carwash did a great job. I explained what had happened and the guys took care of everything, even under the hood. When I got home, Jeff looked outside and said, "Wow. The car looks great. You had it cleaned? What's the occasion?"

The car had been pretty dirty, with salt from the road and dried slush and other winter residue. We never had the car cleaned; we'd just wait for it to rain. I thought a moment and said, "I think I need to tell you something."

I told him about the blood, but I couldn't bear to say it was from our rabbit, so I told him it was a possum. I told him about Marie's tires. I told him about Jeanine and Tom's hedges. I still didn't think it was a good idea to tell him about the stalker, so I left that part out.

"I was wondering what happened to their hedges. My God. Why didn't you tell me this before?"

"You had a lot going on. I didn't want to add to your stress."

"I can't believe you all were going through that. I'm so sorry. Do the police have any idea who's responsible?"

"So far, no. They're working on it."

"Let me drive you to work tomorrow. And I'll give you a ride home. Sounds like you can use a break."

He could say that again.

"This has gone too far," Dr. Osgood said. "Although, I have to give you points for telling Jeff."

Looked like I wouldn't flunk therapy this week.

"Maybe they'll stop now that Jeff knows," I said. "If it's even them."

"Let's talk about this. Who else could it be?"

"Well, I think Plaid Guy is definitely them. But slashed tires? The rabbit? I don't know."

"You just had a Reliability Assessment, which raised some red flags. Keep in mind, this group can be very aggressive. Assume the vandalism is them."

"What I can't figure out is, how did they know about our rabbit? How did they know where to find it? That couldn't have been by chance." I was obsessed by this rabbit thing. I saw the look on her face and decided to drop it. "I suppose I could just give in and start Tier Training.

One session. How much could that cost?"

"They won't let you pay for just one session."

"You sound like you know something about this...."

Dr. Osgood looked down at her notes. "Okay. I suppose I should have told you...."

Now what? She paused a long time before she spoke again. She took off her glasses.

"I have a sister who was a Philomathist."

"Was?"

She waited. I thought maybe she was trying to decide whether she should be telling me this.

"When she tried to leave, they did everything they could do to intimidate her."

"But I'm not even one of them. I just dabble, to know what Jeff's getting into."

"You're one of them. You do assessments."

"What if I stop?"

"They already consider you to be part of the Church. You may not be involved enough for their liking, but the harassment, the stalker, Floyd on your doorstep, just trying to keep you in line. They want to ensure you're not going anywhere."

I hadn't considered that I was a Church member. I'd been telling myself I wasn't.

"I'm one of them?"

"That's how they think. People who join are forever theirs. You're their property."

"So, they're the Borg?"

She looked at me with a perplexed look on her face. She didn't know the reference. Maybe I was flunking therapy.

"I want you to consider one more thing," she said.

"Okay..."

"If they figure out who your therapist is... who my sister is... they won't like it."

This put some things in perspective. If the Church did know who her sister was, it would explain some of the cloak-and-dagger stuff.

Breezie had been busy screwing up other projects, so Laura and I had a reprieve. We were working on some mood boards when Tamara entered our room.

"Don't let Discordia see you," I said. "You know she doesn't like her subordinates to commingle."

"Well, Gucci won't have to worry about me anymore," Tamara said. "I wanted you guys to know first. I got hired by Wild Fire."

"In the City?" I said.

"Yeah, midtown. I'm on my way to give Anton my notice."

"Oh my God. Tamara, that's fantastic," Laura said.

"You're leaving and not taking us with you?"

Tamara laughed. "Don't worry. As soon as I'm settled, you'll both be getting a call."

Breezie entered the room, and we quickly shut up. She glared at Tamara.

"Don't you have something else to do?"

Tamara smiled. "Yes," she said, and walked out.

"What do you want, Breezie?" I said. Tamara's news was somehow making me less than polite.

"Just checking on you."

"We're fine. We just started. You can come back later

and see what we're doing."

Somehow, that worked. She nodded and left. If I had known it was that easy, I would have been rude to her a long time ago. Laura threw me a conspiratorial look and smiled broadly.

"What are we going to do without Tamara?" I said. "Anton is going to be really upset."

"If he's smart."

"Right. If he's smart."

"Hey, have you thought about a color scheme?"

"Oh... Yeah. I was thinking we could pick up some of the deep red from that fabric pattern we were looking at yesterday, maybe use some of the cream color that's in it as well. Maybe run with that. We'll keep the furniture's wood framework natural."

I was having trouble focusing. I knew Tamara was only the first deserter; others were sure to follow. For some reason, Anton was blind to Breezie's effects on his staff, and since I knew he wasn't sleeping with her, I could think of no possible explanation for his myopia.

I was suddenly restless. "You know, I'm going to get some coffee. Want some?"

"Yes. Just milk, no sugar, please."

Laura was someone who was entitled to coffee.

I was thinking about what Dr. Osgood said about her sister. This, of course, made me want to find out who, exactly, her sister was.

I started where everyone starts: the internet. People Search, to be exact. They often listed relatives, or possible relatives. I went into my home office, turned on my computer, and searched for my therapist, Dr. Janice Osgood. I found her, but I had to pay a couple bucks to get her full bio. I PayPal'd the fee and got her information. Funny; there wasn't a list of relatives. All they had listed was her husband, Cecil Craigg.

I spent an hour on other search sites, but nothing was coming up other than her name, occupation, and current address.

Something wasn't right.

I decided to check one of the pay sites, one that listed legal notices, criminal records, everything. It had a monthly fee, which I could cancel once I was done. And I hit pay dirt:

Dr. Janice Osgood, née Sara Walsh.

I googled Sara Walsh, and boom! Hundreds of hits. There were lists of relatives, addresses, legal notices, newspaper articles, all sorts of information.

Dr. Osgood—Sara—had pressed charges and filed a civil suit against the Church of Philomathics for harassment while she was an undergrad at Stony Brook University. (Her father, it turned out, was a lawyer. I spent a lot of time on this.) She accused the Church of following her, spying on her, and terrorizing her, simply because she wanted to leave. Among examples cited were a guy in a plaid jacket and goggles following her all over campus; people in hazmat suits continually coming to her dorm room to intimidate her; the word "CROW" spray-painted on the side of her car, and the tires slashed. I thought the worst was when her family dog was stolen, then left, a week later, tied to the parking sign outside one of the buildings where she took class, a threatening note pinned to his collar.

The Church was found guilty, and Sara also won her civil suit. The Church had to pay both legal fines and damages to Sara. She graduated from Stony Brook that year, but there was no more information about her after that. The only other information was about Janice.

While People Search had Dr. Osgood's (and therefore, Sara's) current address in Mineola, the paid search site had Sara's last known address as her dorm room in Stony Brook, NY.

I needed to hear more about this. Was this what Jeff and I had to look forward to, continuous harassment? Looked like I had a few things to discuss with Dr. Osgood next time I saw her.

I had to turn the sound on my phone back on. I was starting to get calls about work. The calls from the center were usually all-zero numbers, anyway, and I gave them a different ring tone so I could tell which ones were theirs without looking. Most of the work calls were for freelance, a month or two at a time, hired-for-the-project kind of jobs. That worked well for my current situation. I called the ones that I thought I could manage with a full-time job and a part-time Jeff problem.

As usual, somehow people knew my business without me telling them. I was at my desk, rendering sketches, when Breezie came up to me and said, "So, Melody. You're freelancing?"

What, was everybody trailing me? Didn't I rate a little privacy? I played it cool.

"When would I have time to do that?"

"I don't know how you're doing it, and I'm sure Anton would love to know, too."

"So would I," I said. My word against hers.

She smiled that fake smile of hers and walked away. If she did tell Anton, he never brought it up with me.

I discussed this with Laura later, when we had a moment to ourselves.

"Breezie thought you were freelancing?"

I smiled. "I am freelancing. Just started."

"How does she know?"

"Maybe she's married to Mr. Plaid Jacket. I have no idea. I think she was calling my bluff."

"What did you say?"

"That I had no time to freelance."

"Does that mean you're leaving, too?"

"I don't know. I'm just getting an idea of what's out there. I'm only taking really small projects. Besides, this will help with my credit-card bills."

"You can't leave. Then I'll have to take down Breezie by myself."

"Just don't look in her eyes when you're ready to lop off her head."

I was getting in my car the next morning, put my bag on the seat, and looked over at the Giordanis' house. My stalker was looking in their window.

I thought maybe he had been reassigned because he hadn't been around much lately, but there he was, on Jeanine's porch. It was a futile endeavor. Jeanine and Tom were already out for the day.

On my way to work, I stopped at the diner to get a donut and coffee. When I got out of the car, he was leaning on the wall of the store next door, eating a muffin.

When I got to work, he was standing in the parking lot.

I went out to lunch with Laura, and he was sitting at the bar of the restaurant.

I was leaving the parking lot, and he was sitting on the curb.

When I got home, Floyd was sitting on my steps.

I wanted to tell Floyd to call off Plaid Guy. However, letting him know I knew the Church had sent this guy to spy on me didn't seem like the best move. I was still trying to recover from that Reliability Assessment. This was not the time to anger Floyd. The Church had already done enough damage. I was hoping they might take a breather.

The next day, Jeff was getting ready to go to the center. He looked good, sounded good. He took a shower (of course), and then I sat there and watched him get dressed. He kept smiling at me as I did, and finally said, "Like what you see?"

"Oh, yes."

Watching him lustfully was not enough to keep him home, however. He kissed me and said, "My car's here. Let's plan on a date tonight."

Better than nothing. I watched him run down the stairs.

"Curses, foiled again," I said aloud, and made myself laugh. What was that from? Snagglepuss? Daffy Duck? Some classic cartoon.

Marie wanted to talk to me, so I agreed to have lunch with her near my office. I didn't think there'd be anything else that would surprise me about this Church, this gang of thugs.

We waited to start talking until our food arrived. The waitress delivered two enormous sandwiches and two oversized drinks.

"I discovered an article about your plaid-jacket friend."

"Oh?"

"He's a member of the Spy Patrol. Apparently, they all have to wear these plaid jackets, knit caps, and goggles. They're supposed to be visible, to send a message. They want you to know you're being watched, to keep you in line."

I practically choked on my soda. "So, there are lots of these guys? Like roaches?"

"Seems to be." Marie was trying to pick up half of her sandwich, but it was so huge she gave up and decided to cut it.

"Well, that explains the other day. That guy was everywhere. I couldn't understand how he did it."

"You're right though," she said. "Their only purpose is to watch and collect data. They aren't supposed to approach you."

There's a term in font design: Tight, not touching. That was these guys.

"Well, they are getting on my last nerve. If that's their objective, they're nailing it."

She finished sawing apart her sandwich and picked up a section.

"Now, the vandalism; that's a different group: The Faction. The Church sends them to Contrary Persons who are interfering with a member's progress. Also, to anyone they think is in danger of quitting."

"I'm not a Contrary Person. Although, Floyd did threaten me once for interfering with Jeff's studies...."

"He threatened you?"

"Not in so many words. Actually, yeah, in so many words."

"Well, that explains some of the harassment."

"Also, I flunked that Reliability Assessment. They didn't like that at all."

I felt a little barbarian, chomping down on my sandwich while Marie demurely picked up each surgically divided quarter of hers.

"In a way," she said, "it makes sense that they would come after Jeanine and me, although it's unsettling that they know we've been talking about them. It's not like we've gone public."

"They just know things. I don't know how they do it."

"Must be their psychic abilities."

I laughed. "Or their psychotic paranoia. Maybe they just go after any potential threat, and most of the time, they get lucky. And if they happen to be wrong, they don't care."

Marie looked out of the window. "Speak of the Devil.... Guy in a plaid jacket, leaning against that blue Toyota."

"Oh, man. Wish I had a giant can of Raid." I got up, went outside, and when he saw me coming towards him, he ran.

"Scat! Shoo!"

When I got back to the table, Marie was laughing.

"They should call themselves the Roach Invasion," I said, and Marie laughed harder. "Really."

I had an appointment to see Dr. Osgood the next morning. I didn't know how she would react, but I was determined to find out about her and the Church.

I decided just to be upfront.

"How's it going?" she asked.

"I tried to find your sister."

"Oh?"

"It seems you don't have one."

She thought a moment. "No, I don't," she said.

That made me laugh. "So, you were a Philomathist in college?"

She sighed.

"Briefly, yes. I was a psych major and thought it sounded interesting... until I found out they were opposed to both medicine and psychology."

"When did you change your name?"

"After the trial. I should never have let my father sue them, but I didn't know that at the time. Because I was so young, there was a lot of publicity, and, even when we won, instead of stopping, the Church got even more aggressive. They wouldn't leave me alone. And I didn't think they ever would."

This didn't bode well for Jeff and me.

"Still," I said, "I'm surprised they couldn't find you. I did."

"After I changed my name, I moved to California and got a P.O. Box, which was under yet a different name. Realize, there was no Google then. I stayed out there until I finished my doctorate in psychology. Ironically, the money from the suit paid for my graduate degrees. I guess by the time I moved back east, they had given up trying to find me."

I was wishing Google had never been invented.

"Any other questions?" she said with a smile. "Or did you want to spend your whole hour on my past life?"

"Just one thing. Do you think the Church will ever leave Jeff and me alone?"

She frowned. "To tell you the truth, I really don't know.... Do you plan on suing them?"

"No."

"Well, I don't know what they'll do. But I'm hoping you'll fare better than I did."

That wasn't very encouraging. I left Dr. Osgood's office unsatisfied. I went down the elevator to street level, walked out of the building, and there, right in front of me, were three Spy Patrol guys, leaning against the three cars parked across from the entrance. They were miming "See No Evil, Hear No Evil, Speak No Evil." My heart jumped right into my throat.

"Tight, not touching...," I said under my breath. I made a wide berth, and slowly walked around them.

I was getting a steady stream of calls for work. I had to say no to a lot of them; they would require more time than I could reasonably afford. But then there was the call from IKEA.

"We would like you to come in for an interview."

Yes! Yes! I'll come in now! Yes! But I calmly said, "Sure? When?"

The interview was on a work day, so I told Gemini I'd be in late. Hicksville was the lesser IKEA, in my opinion:

smaller, smaller parking lot, less stuff, more crowded. It was still IKEA, though.

James Santini, their Design Manager, shook my hand and said, "Welcome." I was hoping he'd say it in Swedish, but unlike everyone else in my life, he couldn't read my mind. I sat down, and he looked over my portfolio.

"This is very impressive. You've done some beautiful work."

"Freelancing provided a lot of diverse experience. But I've been with Gemini Design for about eight years now."

"And why are you interested in IKEA?"

I smiled. "Are you kidding? Mostly, I love the design solutions. But also, I've heard this is a great company to work for."

"You work for a design studio with high-end clients, and you love IKEA?"

"Yes. Not every piece of furniture has to be made out of black walnut trees."

He laughed. I hoped that was a real laugh, not just to humor me.

We discussed design trends, we discussed work environments, we discussed flex hours, we even briefly discussed the Knicks. He closed my portfolio, looked over my resumé again, and said, "Well. I think you'd make a great addition to our team. Let me just ask you: Would you ever have any interest in opportunities in Europe?"

The shock on my face said it all. He laughed.

"Your job skills would be perfect for one of our Senior Interior Designer positions."

"Er... in Europe?"

"This could be something to consider down the road. I'd be thrilled if you came on as the Creative Manager here, for now."

"Uh, wow." I had lost all ability to communicate effectively.

"There are a few more people I still need to interview, and then we'll make our decision. We'll be making calls in the next couple of weeks."

When we were done, I took my own tour of the current showroom. I hadn't been to an IKEA for a while, since before Jeff got sick. The other thing about IKEA: Unlike my own designs, I could afford this furniture.

I was tempted to jump up and click my heels on the way out, not that I knew how. A cartwheel also would have come in handy. I didn't know if I'd go to work there or not, but it was sure nice to feel wanted.

The Faction had been quiet; too quiet, as they say. I started to look out for them again. Thing is, how do you look out for a sneak attack? I thought now that they had done their worst—hoping that killing our rabbit was the worst—that maybe they would just forget about me. I worried about it for about a week, then I put it out of my mind.

I was in the market, went outside, and every grocery cart available was surrounding my car. Just try to move 50 carts away from a car when you're holding two bags of groceries. The store workers came out and started yelling at me, as if I put all the carts around my own car.

"Why would I do this to myself?" I asked them. "I want to leave, and I can't get near my car."

Somehow, the logic sunk in, and they muttered an

apology. I sat on the curb and waited while they moved the carts back to their rightful place in front of the store.

Another call I got was Todd, from Maplewood. I didn't realize I had sent my resumé there; it was a blind application. I'm not sure that loyal me would have applied if I had known.

"We were thrilled to see that you sent in your resumé." Todd was absolutely delighted that I was there.

"Thank you. You know, I didn't even know it was your company."

"So, can I ask: Why are you leaving Gemini?"

He went right to the point.

"I'm seeing what's out there. I might not be leaving; depends on what I find."

"Uh-huh. And have you found anything interesting yet?"

"Possibly one thing, but not much else."

"Well, we know you know our style, because you've worked on so many projects with us. We consider this to be a perfect fit."

"You know I have scheduling issues, right? Would it be a problem if I worked flexible hours? Gemini lets me make up hours on the weekends."

"We understand your situation. We can accommodate your schedule."

He was acting like this was a done deal, and it was making me nervous.

"Would I be working with Gemini? That might be awkward."

"We have other vendors. We can put you on other projects."

"Wow. This is a little overwhelming."

He smiled. "We'll be interviewing other people, but I wanted to talk to you first. Think about it. We should be making calls sometime next week."

Was Maplewood going to steal me out from under Gemini's nose? Was I going to let them?

If Gemini continued to give Breezie more power, I'd say yes.

Now that I knew that Plaid Guy was possibly several Plaid Guys, I was more unnerved. Who knew where they were, what they were watching, what they knew? This explained why the Church seemed to know everything I did. Their eyes were everywhere.

I was thinking again about that poor rabbit. Since the Plaid Guy was actually an infestation of Spy Patrol roaches, it made sense that they might have seen the bunny around and may have seen Jeff and me watching him. Those guys could have been anywhere, even when I didn't notice them.

Floyd had been scolding me again about not doing enough assessments. Apparently, people did them a lot more often than I did, sometimes more than once a day. I did one a month, tops. I had been putting off doing another one, but I decided I'd better make an appointment. I had to keep up appearances.

I was about to call the center, but then I stopped. I was having a horrifying epiphany.

The stupid assessments.
That's how they knew about the rabbit.
I told them about it.

11

On the day I met Jeff's parents, Long Island's meteorological conditions were the worst in its history. Okay, maybe not the worst, but I'm sure everyone who had to travel on that Christmas day was doing a lot of cursing. It wasn't the amount of snow that was the problem. It was the nature of the snow. It was sludgy, heavy, dripping, despicable snow. Snow in Long Island would often fall from the sky like that, not landing as soft, fluffy flakes, but rather splatting on the ground in soggy, grayish chunks.

I was aware that meeting his parents would be an indication to them that we were getting serious. We were, in fact, planning on moving in together; though, I didn't think he'd mentioned that to them yet. Their first impression of me was going to be of an awkward woman in an ugly parka, shaking icy water off her back like a dog, and traipsing black slush all over their perfect home. For a split second, I considered taking off my winter garments before I entered the house but decided that would be too peculiar, even for me.

Jeff opened the door to the house without ringing the doorbell.

"Hello. We're here."

Marie came running in from the other room. She was dressed impeccably: nice red-tone paisley dress, flats, carefully drawn on makeup. She was right out of a 50s homemakers' magazine. "Jeff. Look at you. How's my handsome son?"

Her handsome son was a bag of melting ice cubes.

"I don't know about him, but I'm fine." He took off his drenched coat and hung it on the built-in coatrack in the foyer. I followed his lead.

He hugged and kissed Marie, then said, "Mom, this is Melody."

I was trying to get my boots off without tripping over myself. I reached out to shake her hand, forgetting that my hands were cold and clammy.

"Nice to meet you," I said. Boots off, no falling.

"Hello, dear. Welcome."

Frank came out of the kitchen to say hello, and Marie went to get us something to drink. Unlike his wife, Frank was dressed casually in a sweater and jeans. He was a big guy, taller than Jeff and heavier, but one could see where Jeff got his good looks. We sat down on one of their oversized, plush couches. My feet dangled over the edge.

"So, Jeff, how's the job search?"

"Got some good leads. I really liked one of the stations I saw. Maybe they'll like me. We'll see."

Marie came in with the drinks.

"And Melody," Frank said. "What do you do?"

"I'm a designer."

Marie perked up. "Oh? Do you design clothes?"

"No. I'm an interior designer."

"Well, don't look at our house, then. It's embarrassing."

Of course, the house was beautiful. Big-patterned blue and white curtains, oversized, comfy furniture, gold and mirrored accent tables. I personally went for something more modern, clean lines and all of that, but she did have great taste.

"You have a wonderful house," I said. I was careful not to say "lovely;" I found that condescending. There was a live Christmas tree in the corner, decorated with antique glass ornaments, a silver ribbon that ran top to bottom, and white Christmas lights.

"And your tree is amazing," I said.

"Thank you, dear," she said, then turned to Jeff. "Guess who I ran into the other day? Helen."

I could have guessed that.

"Oh? How is she?"

"She's single again." She lowered her voice to relate this piece of information. "She said she ran into you a while ago. You were going to call her, but you never did."

"No. We said we should be in touch. She could have called me if she was anxious to get together."

"I think it would have been better manners for you to call her, but...."

"Mom, I have no reason to call her. Helen and I aren't even really friends anymore."

"Don't say that. You'll always be friends."

Jeff looked at me and smirked.

"She's at her parents' house for Christmas. I think you

should call her."

"Okay, Mom, we'll see."

I pictured Helen entering Marie's house. She'd be wearing a white snow-bunny jacket and white boots that repelled dirt and moisture. Her perfect white gloves would slide off her hands, which of course would be warm and dry, and when she put down her hood, every strand of her golden hair would be in place.

No, I had no problem with Helen.

Marie had roasted a turkey with cornbread stuffing, yams, green bean casserole, and dinner rolls. Frank made plates for everyone and passed them around.

"Melody," Marie said. "Where do you work? Any place we'd have heard of?"

"I freelance at the moment. I have a contract with a small design studio in Suffolk County."

"Freelance. So, nothing permanent."

"Mom," Jeff said, "her business is a little different than most jobs. A lot of designers freelance."

She frowned. "I see. And Jeff tells me you two met in a bar?"

"Well, actually, I'm not much of a drinker." This was true, but I don't know why I said that. Maybe because of the intensely disapproving glare I was getting from Marie. "My friends and I like to go to this little place that has live music on the weekends. That's where we met."

The conversation paused there. Sounds of people scraping plates and chewing filled the room. Jeff smiled at me and rubbed my leg with his.

"So, tell us, Melody," Marie said, trying to break the silence. "What do your parents do?"

"My parents? Oh. My father was a math professor at

Adelphi."

"That's interesting. And your mother?"

"She was a painter. She taught art at Oyster Bay High School."

"Are they retired now?"

"Uh... deceased. They died in a car accident when I was in my twenties."

"Oh." Marie's expression changed. "I'm sorry, dear."

"Thanks," I said. I never knew what to say to people. That was then almost ten years past.

"Do you have any siblings?"

"An older brother. He's a banker."

Jeff smiled at me and rubbed my leg again.

"Anyway, Jeff," Marie said. "Helen and her family will be at midnight Mass tonight, if you two want to go."

Jeff and I never went to Mass. I looked at him.

"Uh, no, I think we'll pass tonight. Are you and Dad going?"

"Well, if you two aren't going, Dad and I can go to Mass tomorrow morning."

"We're okay here, if you want to go."

"No, we'll go tomorrow."

We all went back to not talking. I looked around the table. Jeff and his parents were looking down at their plates. I wondered if Jeff would have gone to Mass if I wasn't there, especially since Helen was going. I felt I was ruining their little family outing.

In retrospect, Marie was trying. We just didn't have any kind of history, and she and Helen did. These days we had a lot to talk about. And to Marie's credit, she stopped mentioning Helen in front of me.

Jeff came home after a day of training with Floyd Face and that weird plastic smile. I thought I'd better feed him and hoped the effects of the training would wear off.

I decided to try something.

"So, how was the training?"

He looked at me, surprised. He moved his fork around in the Chinese food until he got a decent forkful.

"I've only made it to Tier 3. All this special attention I'm getting and I'm not moving up very quickly"

"How many tiers are there?"

"Twelve," he said, and grinned at me. "I have a ways to go."

"And what happens when you get to Tier 12?"

"Oh, I'm not sure. After that's the really advanced stuff. I know that in the upper Tiers people have recalled past lives, and some can move objects with their thoughts, or make lights turn on and off, things like that."

"Floyd seems pretty advanced. Nothing seems to faze him."

Jeff went back to playing with his food, and said, "Floyd's at Tier 8. I'm nowhere near there yet. Everything seems to bother me. I mean, I've been at this a while, and, other than the immediate high I get from the assessments, I don't feel much progress. I should be further along. I don't want to wind up failing the Pathway."

I didn't know one could fail the Pathway. Maybe that information came with that Tier training I'd been avoiding. Since I'd been crawling along rock bottom, much like a crab, I guessed failing the Pathway wasn't really an issue for me.

"You'll get there," I said.

He smiled and said, "Thanks for asking. I know all this is hard on you."

You don't know the half of it. But I said, "Yeah."

There was something that was going right in my life. My freelance clients were pleased with me and were giving me more work. They had me mostly doing ads, a week's worth, sometimes a month's worth, at a time. I could do this print work stuff in my sleep, which, considering how little time I had for sleep these days, might have had to be the way I did it.

I was working in my home office and heard a noise against the side of the house. I looked up, and there was one of those Spy Patrol guys. Damn it, they really were like cockroaches. What on earth did they want from me? *See? I'm working. I'm not calling anyone. I'm not writing emails to the newspaper. It's just me.*

I got up and banged on the window. He went away.

Talk about being fazed. This was really getting to me. How did people do those reality TV shows where cameras were on them all the time? I had a few spies following me around, and I was becoming unglued.

When Jeff came home, he settled in the window. I had come to the understanding that Jeff might never get any better than he was. He had become a functioning depressive, which was better than never getting out of bed, I supposed. I did miss the old Jeff. I liked having someone to laugh with. I missed feeling I could say anything about anything. But the part of him that was still here was better than his being completely gone. Maybe he'd ultimately fail Philomathics, and we could all go back to normal, whatever that was.

Over the weekend, I was outside filling the birdfeeders. It had been a fairly brutal winter, and I was trying to do this more regularly. Considering how many birds were showing up, they seemed to appreciate it. I had just hung up with Marie, but when I got inside, she called me back.

"Marie. What's going on?"

"I have six men in plaid jackets sitting on my lawn. What do I do with them?"

"Serve them hot cocoa and cookies?"

"Really..."

She sounded upset. She didn't possess my appreciation for the absurd.

"Seriously, if you just open your door, they'll go away."

"They will?'

"Oh, yeah."

"Can you hold on?"

I heard her put down her phone. She walked over to her door and opened it. Then I heard her come back.

"You're right. They ran."

"It's odd that they sent you a half dozen of them, but you and I did meet in public recently."

"I can't wait for this to be over."

"Me too."

After I hung up, I found myself thinking about Floyd. Here was a guy who had no idea he was creating evil. He honestly thought, somewhere in his twisted, reeducated mind, that, not only was what he doing meritorious, it was for the good of all mankind. The fact that he might be badly mistaken never entered his thoughts.

Then we had Breezie, who was a completely different kind of contemptible. She relished being evil. Had no thoughts about doing good for the world, or for anybody in it. She was a marvel to behold. Both of them seemed to be happily plodding along, with no self-doubts to confuse matters. I'd say something trite, like we should all be more like that, but no one should be like Floyd or Breezie.

Monday morning, I was having an annoying conversation with Breezie (is there any other kind?) when my cell phone rang. I let it go to voicemail, not wanting to be rude, even to Breezie. Then I heard it ring again, and though I didn't answer it, I got worried.

"Excuse me, Breezie. I just want to make sure this isn't about Jeff."

Not about Jeff. The first call was IKEA. The second, Maplewood. Breezie was standing over me as I checked my phone.

"Problem?"

"No," I said, and put my phone back in my bag. "Two calls, two separate people."

I went out at lunchtime and sat in my car to call them back. I called IKEA first.

"Melody. Thanks for getting back to us so fast. Listen, we'd like to make you an offer."

The call with Maplewood was about the same, almost word for word. Maplewood was offering more money, but not enough to make the decision easy. I told both of them I'd get back to them by the end of the week.

I sat in my car and pondered my options. IKEA would

be a different, less creative, experience. However, there didn't seem to be any of that high-end competition going on there like I would see at Maplewood. On the other hand, Maplewood would upset Anton more, and did I really want to stop creating upmarket design?

I'd have to discuss this with Jeff when I got home.

I saw Helen again at the center. I could tell she had just finished a Tier Training session, because she was exhibiting Floyd Face. Her zombie gaze broke when she saw me.

"Melanie!"

"Hi, Helen. What's going on?"

"I just got my blue jacket!" She held up the jacket, which was wrapped in plastic, like from a dry cleaner.

"Congratulations. How did you get one?"

"I made it to Tier 2. I had a choice of tasks. I didn't want to be a full-time assessor, so I volunteered to be a greeter. And I got a jacket."

"Well, that's perfect for you."

"Thank you!"

She was already at Tier 2? She got there awfully fast. Jeff was still at Tier 3. And I knew he didn't have a blue jacket.

When I got home, I called Marie.

"Did you know Helen has joined the Church?"

"What? No!"

"Yeah. I've seen her there a few times. I thought you probably knew." *Because everybody knows everything and there are no secrets in my life.*

"Jeff recruited her?"

"Sounded like he mentioned it to her, and she joined. There wasn't much effort involved."

There was silence on the other end of the line, then, "I should talk to her."

"Why? She seems happy. Thrilled, even."

"Because... I want to make sure she isn't thinking that by doing this she'll get back with Jeff."

Nice to know someone thought like me.

"She's flying through the Tier Training," I said. "Says she's at level 2."

"Well... maybe she truly likes it. I still should talk to her."

"By the way... she thinks my name is Melanie."

Marie laughed. "Okay. I won't burst her bubble."

The next morning, I wasn't in the office more than ten minutes when Carol from HR entered the design department. She almost never came into our territory; she usually stayed in her lair on the other side of the floor. I personally never had any problems with Carol. It was just that her appearance was usually the harbinger of the Apocalypse.

Today was no different. She was carrying pink slips. Everybody scattered, except me. There was no point in running. It wasn't like, if she couldn't find someone, that person wouldn't get fired.

She walked up and down the aisles, a malicious Santa delivering bad tidings. She made her way over to me. I looked up from my computer and said, "Hi, Carol."

"Hi, Melody. Tell me. Do you know where Laura sits?"

I was crushed. "Seriously Carol? They're firing Laura?"

"Not firing; laying off. They're laying off all the junior designers."

"Pretty much the same thing." I could let myself be angry at Carol, but this wasn't her decision. "Well, you'll have to find her yourself. I'm not playing Judas today."

"I understand," Carol said.

Something about this wasn't making sense. As Carol turned away, I called her back.

"Listen. I can't believe Anton would lay off all the junior designers. There are a lot of projects in house right now."

"This wasn't Anton's decision. It was Breezie's."

"Breezie?"

"She's the new Art Director."

Of course. These layoffs reeked of Breezie. Stupid twenty-something design neophyte being made Art Director. What was Anton thinking?

What did Jeff say about the Devil? Well, she may have won the battle, but I was determined to win the war.

Laura took her layoff better than I did.

"I'll find another job. Roger is working, and there are a couple of studios I've already sent resumés to. Something will come up."

We were sitting on the curb in the office parking lot, pretending it wasn't February. They had escorted Laura down the elevator with the other pink-slip recipients. The others had already cleared out.

She saw the look on my face.

"Really. I'll be fine."

I looked up. "Oh, fuck."

"What?"

"One of those Plaid Guys. Over there." I stood up. "I'm going to talk to that weasel."

"Melody—" Laura called out.

I didn't want to be talked out of it. I crossed the parking lot. This guy had picked the wrong day to mess with me. He was leaning against someone's car and looked up just as I approached him. He put his cell phone in his pocket and looked like he wanted to run, but I had him cornered.

"No, you don't. You stay right there."

He stopped and looked at me.

"C-can I help you?"

"Yes. You can tell Floyd that I'm on to you, and you can stop following me."

"What... uh... what do you mean?" he stuttered. He appeared to be afraid of me. This guy was not a professional.

"Just tell him."

I walked back to the curb.

"That was amazing," Laura said.

It occurred to me that maybe he wasn't afraid of me at all. He was probably afraid of Floyd.

"Either it was, or I just made a very, very, big mistake."

As I headed back into the building, I was finding I was angrier about the layoffs than I should have been. I felt the only recourse to this situation was to leave, and I was already going to do that. It was just a matter of making a decision. So, I made one.

This would be considered an impulsive, all right.

I stopped just outside of the building, called IKEA, and got a start date.

I had envisioned a dramatic exit, with furniture being overturned, yelling, and screaming, with a big fuck you to Breezie, like that. But as I went back inside the office, I decided simple timing would be dramatic enough.

I went into Anton's office.

"Hi, Melody. What's up?"

I closed the door.

"I'm giving my notice."

Why he hadn't seen this coming was astounding. But then he got patronizing; ooh do I hate that.

"It's your husband, huh? Things aren't going well?"

There's a fine line between being understanding and being condescending. I held it together. No reason to call him out on being a putz.

"No. I've got another offer. I start in three weeks."

There. That was the look on his face I wanted to see.

"Oh... Well, can I ask why you want to leave?"

"It's a better job. Also, frankly, I hate working with Breezie."

There. Someone had to say it.

"I thought you said you could work with her."

"I can. I can work with anyone. But, I'd rather not. Anton, she's awful. She's cruel to the junior designers, she's rude to the senior designers, she's not up for the job, she takes credit for other people's work...." I could've gone on, but I decided to stop there.

"That seems like a petty reason to leave a job."

I scowled. Of course, he would think that. "No. You put a twenty-something novice who treats people like crap in charge. But it doesn't matter to me anymore. I won't be here."

I stood up to leave. Anton stood up too and said, "Can I ask where you'll be going?"

"No."

"Well, can I make you a counteroffer?"

I thought a moment. A counteroffer. Money? Was that the reason I was leaving? "No," I said, and left his office.

I knew my leaving would not change anything at Gemini. It was the New Order. They weren't about to go back to the Old Order. My leaving wouldn't make Breezie any less obnoxious or help anyone get out from under her thumb. The only thing it might do was give Breezie fewer design ideas to steal. Maybe I was letting her win, but in my book, this was a coup for Melody.

Although Laura would know where I was going, I had no intention of telling anyone else where to find me. Everyone was asking me, even Breezie. Another reason to have picked IKEA. If I had gone to Maplewood, everyone would have known where I was.

12

Breezie, of course, was happy; triumphant, even. I avoided her. I was just wrapping things up, anyway. I could finish the project Laura and I were doing without anyone else's help, and Anton wisely kept Breezie away from me.

People were approaching me, making sure they had my number, asking where I was going, congratulating me. When Evelyn came up to me, I handed her the business card I got from Maplewood and said, "I told Todd you would call."

There was a part of me that could see that this was admitting defeat, but honestly, this wasn't a battle I cared to win. What would I win? Stay around and watch Breezie treat everyone like dirt? This wasn't my idea of a good work environment. I liked to design. If people were letting me do it, that was a good job. If they weren't, well... I found a place that would.

I got a call from Laura over the weekend. She took a job at a small studio in Garden City. They needed someone to help design and maintain their website, which Laura knew only a little about but was eager to learn. The people were nice, the hours were normal, the commute short. She was right; she'd be fine.

"I'm sorry I missed that you gave notice. Was Anton upset?"

"Yeah. He called me petty."

"He did?"

"I told him Breezie was the reason I was leaving."

"Wow."

I was sitting in my living room while I talked to her. I had been watching John Lennon and Chuck Berry singing Johnny B. Goode from the Mike Douglas DVDs I got from Jeff. I got up to sit in the window, and across the street, was a Spy Patrol guy.

"Oh, look," I said. "Apparently he's still around."

"Who?"

"Plaid Guy."

I got my coat, took my phone outside, and sat on my porch. Sitting in full view would play with Spy Patrol guy's head.

"Okay. I'm outside. I'm going to play chicken with Plaid Guy. See who bails first. Maybe I'll make it to Tier 1."

She laughed. "You're getting daring."

"These guys are just the spies. It's the Faction I have to worry about."

I eventually got bored and went back inside. He was gone by the time Jeff got home.

Saturdays were now Jeff's only set day at the store. The center was getting first crack at him on other days. Marie came over one Saturday afternoon with what she said was interesting information. I made coffee and set out some cookies. I didn't bake them; they were Pepperidge Farm.

"So, whatcha got?"

Marie took a cookie. "Well, Jeff mentioned to me that Floyd was the one he met at the mall the first day he joined the Church."

"Right. So?"

She smiled and sipped her coffee. Whatever she had, it was good. "No one at Floyd's level does those initial anxiety tests. That's considered a lower-Tier job."

"What are you saying?"

"I'm saying, he did something they didn't like, and they punished him."

"Floyd?! Weeny Floyd? Wow. That's intriguing."

"Isn't it?"

"Any idea what?"

"Could be anything. Probably something he said in his Reliability Assessments. Upper Tier people have to do them every six months. He probably admitted to something, and he's making amends. Philomathists believe that full disclosure is part of the Pathway. If it's something really egregious, they fail and have to start all over from day one. Which is a big deal if you're in one of those upper Tiers."

Failing the Pathway. Now I got it. I took a cookie and looked at her. She was grinning like an emoji.

"So. Mr. Peabody and company were displeased with Floyd?" I said. "That's, well, fabulous."

"Thought you could use some good news for a change."

My phone rang. It was the center. I declined the call.

"Who was that?"

"The people at the center."

Marie took another cookie.

"Oh. They're calling now?"

"Oh yeah. They've been calling, every few hours, since my Reliability Assessment. I don't pick up anymore, but they keep at it."

"That's better than a dead animal."

"Any day," I said. "You know, Floyd's penance might not be just sitting outside, getting people to sign up. Maybe this whole thing where he's assigned to Jeff and me is also his punishment."

Marie laughed. "Wow. Poor Floyd."

"Seriously," I said. "And I thought Floyd was our punishment."

Marie had read that Philomathics considered the Tier Training to be the key to bringing people more in tune with their dekan and less trapped in their earthly bodies. If Floyd was at Tier 8, that meant, theoretically, he could do that exercise where he could move forks with his voice, even remember past lives. I sincerely doubted that he could do any of that. Maybe that was why he hadn't progressed any higher.

Jeff was at Tier 3. I remembered from that Tier-Training book I didn't read that that was where the trainer would try to provoke reactions from the trainee. I guessed when they couldn't provoke him anymore, he would go to Tier 4. Then what? Would they throw him in a snake pit? I could just see myself sitting in a room with someone trying to provoke me. I'd take a swing at him.

What did I tell you? Very bad at religions; even worse at cults.

This was the part I didn't understand. What did people think they were going to get from Philomathics? People reportedly paid hundreds of thousands of dollars, often going into tremendous debt, to learn this stuff. If a person wanted to have the feeling of leaving his body, he could just hang with his head upside down for a long time. He'd feel lightheaded naturally. Heightened states, bullshit. Were some people so damaged that they'd believe anything to make it all go away?

The answer, of course, was yes. And cults like Philomathics took advantage of them. They had people looking for magical solutions that simply weren't there. As for my Jeff, he wasn't really getting better. He had something to focus on, but he was still depressed. And I don't mean sad. I mean depressed: low energy, lack-of-will depressed. He wasn't traumatized by some hidden experience; he was clinically ill.

Then, I came to a realization.

I was floating in our oversized tub one Saturday, reveling in the mad bubbles that resulted from my using too much bubble bath. Jeff had gone to the gym and then would be spending the day at the record store. I had the morning to myself, and I was enjoying the quiet when, out of nowhere, I started humming a 70s song by Little Sister.

"*Shady as a lady with a mustache. hmm-hmm hmm-hmm hmm-hmm hmm-hmm HMM. Somebody's watching you....*"

I never did have the rest of the lyrics to that one down. It amused me now that that was what I had going through my head.

"*Somebody's watching you...somebody's watching you-oo. Somebody's watching you...Somebody's watching you-oo.*"

Little Sister was a group fronted by the younger sister of Sly Stone. Its members were the background vocalists for the Family Stone, who recorded the song first. Yes, I had random music trivia in my head. That was what I got for being married to the Billboard 5000.

I got out of the tub, wrapped myself in an oversized bath towel, and, still humming, went into the bedroom. This was going to be an easy Saturday. I wasn't going to run, I wasn't going to work, I wasn't going to cook. I would read something that wasn't Philomathics and listen to music all day, maybe have my way with my husband when he returned home. We could order some Chinese food and stay in. That sounded like a perfect Saturday to me. No Floyd. No Spy Patrol. No Faction. Just us.

I dropped the towel and started to get dressed. I always tried to match the color of my undergarments to my outer garments. I believed only Jeff knew that, although there may have been an ex somewhere who had also figured that out. As I was putting on my jeans, I noticed that Philomathics Tier-Training book, now on top of the pile. I picked it up, sat down, and flipped through it: Acknowledging, Communicating, Challenging, Controlling, Listening.... I suddenly had a moment of resolve. It was big. It was mind-blowing.

I called Dr. Osgood and told her I had to see her.

She couldn't see me until Monday morning. That gave me plenty of time to change my mind, ponder my decision, and change my mind again.

I got to her office early.

"So..." I said. I was afraid to even say it aloud. Dr. Osgood waited.

"I was thinking... I'm going to leave the Church."

Her face was like a three-year-old who had just met Santa. See? I wasn't flunking therapy.

"And how did you come to this decision?"

"I'm not scared anymore."

Dr. Osgood looked at me like I was missing something very obvious.

"What can they do to me they haven't already done? Okay, they'll harass me more. But they can't send the Crow Posse without Jeff knowing about it. Yeah, I thought about this. I'm not going to go public and denounce them or anything. I'm still just a cog in a very big wheel. They won't even notice I'm gone."

She smiled. "Floyd will."

I laughed. "Well, Floyd has issues. Maybe he should be going to more assessments and leave me the hell alone."

"Well, I think that's very brave, and a very good decision."

"At this point, I've spent countless hours reading E. W. Peabody books. I know more than enough to understand what Jeff is going through. That was the point originally, anyway."

When I left her office, I was nervous, and happy, and scared, and relieved, and... well, let's just say, a boatload of emotions were hitting me at once. Step by step, though. I had a whole day of work to get through before I dealt with this.

Floyd was on my porch when I got home. He must have been sitting there a while. It had been drizzling all day, and he was damp and shivering.

Okay. I guessed I would deal with Floyd first.

"Look, Floyd," I said. He didn't look at me, or even toward me. Was he even listening? "I'm... going to stop doing this."

His face was stoic. "You'll be stopping your studies?"

"Yes. Studies. Services. Assessments. All of it. I'm... done."

He looked through me and paused, maybe for effect.

"So, you will not be pursuing the Pathway to Liberation this lifetime?"

Something about the way he said that made me sad. His face changed. Was Floyd exhibiting an emotion?

"No. It's just not for me."

He stared a long time, so long it made me anxious.

"Okay," he said. "Then I encourage you to do an Exit Evaluation."

Or what? People will follow me around, mutilate my neighbors' hedges, slash my mother-in-law's tires?

"What does an Exit Evaluation entail?"

He stood up. "I'll make you an appointment at the center. I'll be in touch."

Floyd didn't like to answer questions. I'd learned that much.

Jeff's ride was pulling up. Floyd waited for him to approach us.

"Well," Floyd said. "Looks like you two have a lot to talk about."

He actually looked directly at me, then at Jeff. I was

beginning to think the man didn't really have eyes. We watched him get into his car and drive off.

"What was that about?" Jeff said.

"Come inside. Let's talk."

He followed me into the house. "What's going on?"

"Well...," I said. I was worried. Floyd was easy; I didn't care what he thought. I waited while Jeff hung up his coat. Yes, I was stalling.

Jeff smiled a Real-Jeff smile. "Come on. It's just me."

"Okay," I said. It was like ripping off a Band-Aid. Just do it. "I've decided to stop studying Philomathics."

He bit his lips and looked serious.

"I see."

Please don't be mad.

He did the Floyd Face thing; his eyes were looking somewhere behind me.

"How long have you been thinking about this?"

The truth was all coming out anyway. "Since I started...."

"Oh."

Look at me, damn it. I'm not one of your assessment subjects.

He was very quiet for a while.

"So, you went through all of this for me?"

"Yes."

He stopped the Floyd Face and looked at me. "Wow. You didn't have to do that."

Was he kidding me? I didn't want to spoil the moment we were having, so I wisely shut up. He kissed me and gave me a Jeff-patented, bear hug.

This feeling of freedom: it had been over two years of this nonsense. I'll show you all the Pathway to Liberation.

Quit fucking Philomathics. My plan was to feed as much anti-Peabody input into my brain as possible. Music, books, newspapers, television. Maybe I would start drinking heavily. I played Jeff's collection of Rolling Stones, including all of the bootlegs. I watched the entire Marx Brothers marathon on TCM. I needed to think about anything else. Philomathics didn't break me, but it did bend me.

If Jeff was upset about my decision, he didn't give me any clues. He was acting no differently. Of course, paranoid me, I wondered if that was what they trained him to do if his wife ever deserted. Meanwhile, I was feeling honest. This was who I was and pretending to be able to stand all those Peabody books was just too much pressure. Finally, I was done.

13

Apparently, no one told the Spy Patrol that I had left the Church. There were two of them sitting on the Giordanis' porch watching me back up my car, and another one at the diner where I picked up my morning coffee. Marie told me there was one sitting on her lawn that morning as well.

IKEA asked me to design a 315-square-ft. bedroom, which was about the size of our master in Floral Park. I drafted a space that would fit the allotted measurements in the showroom, using a queen-sized bed frame, a matching dresser, and a Pax closet system. I tried to make it as different from our bedroom as I could, which was hard, considering our room was also full of IKEA furniture.

The mailroom guy was making the rounds, and when he came into my area, he gave me a box.

"What's this?"

"Dunno. The return address is a P.O. Box. Did you

order something?"

"Not here."

I took my X-Acto knife and cut through the tape. Inside the box were about a dozen rotten apples, crawling with worms.

"Oh, geez!" The smell of rotting apples made me gag. No, it did not smell like apple sauce.

Everyone turned around to look at me.

"What? What is it? Are you okay?"

I wasn't okay. I had left their stupid Church. Couldn't they just leave me in peace? That Exit Evaluation couldn't come soon enough.

It was getting dark by the time I was leaving IKEA. Mine was one of the last cars in the parking lot, and I was a little nervous walking to my car. I reached it without incident. My imagination was just getting the better of me. I turned the key in the ignition, switched on the radio, and slowly navigated across the parking lot to the strains of Sara Bareilles singing "Brave." As I pulled out of the lot, a car came up behind me and started tailgating. This was a serious pet peeve of mine. I immediately pulled over and slowed way down, but the car wouldn't pass. Concerned, I stopped altogether. The other car stopped, too. When the driver didn't get out to approach me, I started up again. He was still right behind me, so I tried accelerating a bit. I was soon exceeding the speed limit, which I never do. When I turned onto the parkway, the tailgater followed, stubbornly stuck to my bumper. I continued on that road, hoping he would give up, but he didn't. He even switched on his high beams. The lights were blazing in my rearview mirror, and I was having trouble focusing on the road ahead of me. I was practically hyperventilating. My fingers were starting to cramp from my iron grip on the steering wheel. There was an egress, and I made a U-turn, joining the oncoming traffic. The vehicle behind me did, too. I pressed on in the opposite direction. The tailgater suddenly knocked against me. I kept control of my car, but now, I was panicking. He hit me again, and my car swerved into the next lane. I righted the car and tried to speed up even more. He banged into me one more time, and then I saw a parkway sign indicating a town that I didn't recognize. I thought I'd better get off the road. I took the exit, which brought me to one of those residential areas with no streetlights. I turned into the first driveway I saw. I was lucky; the other vehicle rushed past.

That was really stupid of me. What if the car had pulled in behind me instead and trapped me? I stayed for some time in the driveway, collecting my thoughts. Then I shut off the radio and called Dr. Osgood.

"Where are you now?"

"Still in the driveway." I was trembling. Those bastards got me good.

"Give me the address."

With no streetlamps, I couldn't see the road signs or the house number. I turned on Siri to find my location, hoping that when I said, "Where am I?" she would be able to tell me with at least some accuracy.

"Got it," Dr. Osgood said. "On my way."

I was completely unraveling. I held my yin-yang necklace and tried to calm down, but every sound outside made me jump. If I turned the radio back on, I wouldn't hear if someone was coming. I decided to hum to myself. Did I know all the lyrics to "A Day in the Life"? "Thunder Road"? "Bridge Over Troubled Water"?

I switched on my parking lights so Dr. Osgood could see me. It seemed like forever, but finally, a car slowly approached, and Dr. Osgood texted me.

"I'm here. I'm going to turn into the driveway."

A car pulled in behind me and flashed its lights. Dr. Osgood got out of the car. I could see her in the headlights. It was the first time I'd ever seen her in jeans. She walked up to my car, and I cracked my window.

"Okay. Let's go. I'll escort you home."

I never thought I'd say this to Dr. Osgood, but I said it. "Thank you."

Dr. Osgood waited for me to get in my house before she left. The lights were on; Jeff was home. I felt safe again.

"What's wrong?" he said.

I must have been visibly shaken. I had to come up with something to say. "I almost got into an accident. Someone... clipped the rear of my car. I had to slam on my brakes."

He hugged me. He was warm and cuddly and Real-Jeff-like. He calmed me right down.

Now they had me spooked. I wanted to call Floyd and tell him off, but I didn't want him to know he was getting to me. There had already been way too much Floyd in my life. Maybe I should have told him the reason I left the Church was because he was so creepy.

I assumed that the brainwashed, hateful humanoid who had been following me was from the Faction. Thing was, I didn't get his license plate, so I couldn't call the police. In New York State, you have to have a plate on the front of your car as well as the back. That's very convenient when you're being followed; except, I was too busy trying to get away from him to read his plate.

I knew that was to scare me, and you know, it did. However, this would be over soon. I had my Exit Evaluation scheduled for the upcoming weekend.

Helen was one of the greeters when I got to the center. All smiles, she asked me who I was there to see. When I said Floyd, she was stunned.

"You're here for an Exit Evaluation? You're leaving the Church?"

"Yes."

Her smile faded, and she got this strange look on her face, like she had suddenly become real.

"I'm so sorry," she said.

I didn't know how to respond to that. She gave me the room number, and I went upstairs. Floyd was waiting for me in one of the private glass rooms. I took hold of the psych device, and we began.

"Why are you leaving?"

That seemed easy enough.

"It's just not for me," I said.

"Did someone talk you into leaving?"

"No, it was my decision."

"Do you have any sexual deviations that would cause you to want to leave?"

"What? No." I should have known Floyd would ask something like that.

"Do you masturbate?"

"I don't have to; I have a husband." I couldn't resist.

"What exactly did you tell your husband as to why you are leaving?"

"I told him what I just told you; it's not for me."

"Are you trying to turn him against us?"

"No."

"Have you been in contact with any Contrary Persons?"

"Uh... no."

"What about your therapist? You are still seeing her, yes?"

There it was. I didn't know what to say. "Well, yes...."

"So, you have been in contact with a CP. Admit you are lying."

"Okay, yes."

"Yes, what?"

"Yes, I was lying."

"Do you have negative thoughts about the Church?

"No."

"The teachings?"

"No."

"E. W. Peabody?"

"No."

It went on for hours. I deflected everything as best I could. Floyd asked me about Jeanine and Marie. He asked me about Tamara, Laura, and their husbands. He asked me what music I listened to, what books I read, what movies I went to. He asked me over and over what kind of sex I liked, what time I went to sleep, even what food I ate. It was insane. I became belligerent. I was tired of answering his stupid questions. What was it he wanted me to say?

"Well," he said when we finally finished. "The results will take a week or two. We'll be in touch."

Results? And then what?

James asked me if I would go with them to visit their Brooklyn store. Brooklyn meant the City, so of course, I said yes.

Jeff was thrilled I had this opportunity.

"You want to come with me?" I said.

"You'll be in meetings all day," he said. "I'll just cramp your style. You and I will go another time."

He was probably right, but I hated to go to the City without him. It felt like I was abandoning him. Then, as it got closer to the day, Jeff started to anchor himself to the window again. Maybe leaving him behind was a bad idea.

"Are you alright?" I said. "Should I not go?"

He smiled. "You have to go. I'm okay here."

It would have been a little more convincing if he wasn't still in his pajamas, in his robe, at six in the evening.

"Well, I'm going to tell Marie to check in on you, just in case."

"I'll be fine. Go. Have a good time."

"Should I leave you the car?"

"No. Take the car. That way you can drive yourself home if it gets late."

What I did do was change my plans of leaving with James and the others the night before and chose to go in the morning. They were staying in a hotel; I didn't need to do that.

I left before Jeff got up. He was sleeping, so I thought

he was probably okay. I stopped at the Dunkin' Donuts by the station, as I was in no hurry to join the huge crowd on the platform. When I walked in, someone said my name. I turned around. Anton was in line, waiting for his coffee.

"Good to see you," he said. "Are you taking a train?"

"Heading to New York for a meeting." That felt good to say.

"I see...." He was avoiding eye contact. "Listen, I owe you an apology."

"You do?" He did, but I wanted to hear him say it. I wasn't going to make this easy for him.

"I'm sorry. I should have listened to you. I tried to work on a project with Breezie, but it turned out she didn't know the first thing about design. I had to let her go."

I could just picture Breezie's smug, ceramic face cracking upon hearing this news. However, even though Anton fired her, Breezie now had a resumé with an Art Director credit. Potential employers would think she had earned it.

"I lost a lot of good people because of her."

I let him squirm.

"Anyway, if you ever want to come back... If it doesn't work out at your new place.... give me a call."

He took his coffee, and the bag that was probably holding a donut, and backed out of the store. When he was gone, I let myself smile.

I forced my way through the mob on the platform and then onto the train. Uncomfortable as I was, I could handle the fact that I would have to stand all the way to New York, sandwiched between the sweaty fat guy in the long coat and the heavily perfumed woman with the cell phone. I clutched my yin-yang amulet and hoped there would be enough air for everyone for the entire ride.

Penn Station was even worse: the pushing, the shoving, the cursing, the begging. I had to get to Red Hook, and since I didn't know where that was, the company had ordered a car for me. I called Marie from the car. She had talked to Jeff. He was up, he was eating, and he was going to the center. I relaxed.

The Brooklyn IKEA was amazing. The building was right on the river, and apparently there was a ferry that went back and forth to lower Manhattan. They had parking spaces under the building, so a shopper could pull right up to the exit doors and load their purchases. The showroom was much bigger than Hicksville, and, along with sample rooms, they also had entire sample apartments, some only 750 square feet, some even smaller. I was introduced to a lot of managers and salespeople. I felt like James was showing me off.

I didn't stay to have dinner with everyone. I left just before the evening rush hour, so the train ride back to the Island wasn't bad. I even got a seat. Earbuds in, I tuned out the passengers and train noise, even the screaming kids.

When I got off the train, Floyd and four blue-jacket stewards were on the platform.

"Melody. We need to talk."

My favorite expression. Right up there with "Let's talk about you." Floyd had a stern look on his iron face. My gut wrenched. What was going on? And how did he know what train I was on?

I knew better than to ponder such a question.

"We have gotten the results of your Exit Evaluation. You have been deemed a CP."

"What? Me? A Contrary Person?" I was perplexed. "I

just want out. I have nothing against you guys. It's just not my thing."

He continued. "You know Jeff has been an excellent addition to our little family at the center. Excellent."

"Well, I'm glad you think so."

"It has been decided that Jeff needs isolating, for his own good. We don't like to break up the family unit, but unfortunately, sometimes it's necessary."

Isolating? Suddenly I understood. Tidal waves of terror crashed down on me. My whole body went into spasms.

"Where's Jeff?"

"Jeff is well. He is going somewhere he can isolate from you. I hope you won't try to follow him. This is for the good of his spiritual growth—his Pathway to Liberation."

I wanted to vomit.

"Say you understand."

I found him so repulsive I couldn't speak.

"Very well." Floyd nodded at me and left me standing on the platform with my mouth hanging open.

I didn't believe Jeff would let them take him away. More importantly, I didn't believe Jeff would pick them over me. I got in my car and rushed home. I didn't care that I was speeding. When I got there, the door was unlocked.

"Jeff? Jeff! Are you home?"

Jeff's suitcase, a lot of his clothes, and all of his E. W. Peabody books were gone. His robe, the one I bought him, was gone. His razor, his toothbrush, practically everything from the medicine cabinet, except maybe my tampons, were gone. A wad of cash we had in the house for mad money was also gone. His keys were on the dresser. His cell phone was there, too, smashed to bits. And there was a typed note, on fancy Church of Philomathics stationary:

"Melody—

Please don't try to find me. Since you are now deemed a Contrary Person, we can no longer be together. I will love you always.

—Jeff."

I fell to my knees in the bedroom and wept.

Jeff was right. The Devil always wins.

14

I woke up in the middle of the night. I was curled up in a fetal position on the carpet in our bedroom, still in my clothes. I had been having nightmares, and I was still shaky and afraid to move. I slowly got up off the floor and saw the clock; it was after three.

I staggered into the bathroom to splash water on my face. My makeup was smeared, and I grabbed a makeup-remover cloth to wipe it off. Then I turned out the light and went into the bedroom.

It was a clear but chilly March night. The moon was almost full; there was bright light streaming in the windows. I undressed and then put on my pajamas. We had extra sheets and blankets in the closet on the other side of the room, and I took one of each and headed downstairs. I threw the sheet over the couch, lay down with the blanket over me, and went back to sleep.

Someone's car alarm went off early in the morning,

forcing me awake. There was a phone call I had to make that I was dreading, but my purse, and therefore my phone, were still upstairs where I had dropped them. I groaned. Make the coffee first, or make the phone call? Time didn't exist yet. I made the coffee.

Poor Marie. I called her, and she became frantic. She said she'd be right over. I figured the day wasn't really going to start until she got there, so I closed the bedroom drapes to block most of the sunlight, put on some clothes, and sat on my bed until the doorbell rang. When I used to meditate, the Transcendental Meditation folks used to tell us to close our eyes, and then they'd ask, "Was there a thought in that silence?" and you were supposed to say, "Yes," because the normal state of humans was to be constantly having thoughts. At that moment, I would have told them, "No, nothing but silence."

Marie arrived, bringing with her all the energy I didn't have. She was going to tackle this crisis at full throttle. She was wearing sweats; I didn't even know she owned sweats. First step: call the police. Two very young police officers arrived, probably expecting us to tell them that the missing person we were reporting was a child. We explained that Jeff had a history of severe depression, which made them a little more understanding. But we kind of knew where he was, so he wasn't exactly a missing person. And he might have been convinced to go voluntarily, so we couldn't say for certain he'd been kidnapped. The officers were very nice, very thorough, but weren't 100% sure how they were going to help us.

They were just leaving when Jeanine and Tom came over from next door.

"What's going on?" Jeanine said. "Why are the police

here? Is everything all right?"

"Jeff is gone," I said, and was a little surprised at how distraught I sounded. "He's being isolated by the Church."

My neighbors looked confused. "Isolated?"

"It's something they do when they want to separate a Church member from someone," Marie said. She reached for Tom's hand. "Hello. I'm Marie, Jeff's mom."

Marie made us all breakfast. I just played with the scrambled eggs on my plate and pretended to butter my toast. My guests spent a few minutes looking at me with concern, then they started discussing what they could do: Hire a private eye, visit different Philomathics centers in the area to see if Jeff was there, join the Church themselves as spies (an idea they all rejected as soon as Tom said it), and of course, more research on the internet.

"We'll find him," Jeanine said.

When everyone left, I called Dr. Osgood; surely this was an emergency. She agreed to see me at her office. I was inconsolable.

"Where do you think they might have taken him?" she said. "Do you think he's at the center?"

"I don't know. Marie said he was planning on going there Friday morning, so probably."

"Well, I would go to the center first and see if he's there."

"Someone must have gone to the house to get his stuff because I don't believe Jeff voluntarily left his keys and broke his own cell phone."

"No, of course not," she said. "There was enough time for him to become despondent. Maybe he just followed their instructions like he's been doing when he gets like that. They probably convinced him they were going to help him."

"I'm sure. Real Jeff wouldn't have blindly chosen to go with them." I took a tissue from the box on the coffee table. I couldn't remember ever crying in her office before. "Did you do that Exit Evaluation thing when you left the Church?"

"No. They told me it was in case I ever wanted to come back, to be in good standing. I told them I never would."

"That's more than Floyd told me." I thought a moment. "I don't know how I'm going to get through this."

"Let's not get ahead of ourselves. You still need to check at the center. In any case, I believe he'll be back. You may have to ride this out, somehow deal with the harassment and the threats. That's what I didn't do, and it was a mistake. It made everything worse."

I forced myself to drive to the center. I was nervous approaching the entrance; it was like it was the first time I'd ever been there. The greeters all stopped what they were doing and watched me walk up to the desk. Even Helen wasn't smiling, and no one spoke. I decided just to say it: "Is Jeff here?"

The greeters were trying to hide behind each other, as if I might be contagious. Helen finally stepped up and said, "Why would he be here?"

Seriously? He's been practically living here. Before I could respond, one of the other greeters pushed her aside and said, "He's not here. Have you tried looking at home? Have you checked the bars?" And then, with much venom, "His girlfriend's house?"

I was a raw nerve, and this put me over the edge. I shrieked, "How can you stand to be so evil?!"

While the Blue Meanies were delighting in my despair,

four other Church members came out of nowhere and surrounded me. One of them put his hands on my shoulders, probably to lead me out, but I shook him off. Then the others grabbed me and forcibly led me out of the center.

"Get your hands off me!"

They dragged me to the exit and left me standing just outside the door.

Too humiliated to go back inside, I went to my car, sat in the front seat, and sobbed. When I finally calmed down, I drove home to my empty house. I took the cushions from the couch and threw them around the room. I fell to my knees and pounded the floor. This wasn't Jeff. It was Them. Evil Them. I would find Jeff. I would do something. I didn't know what, but something. It would take some time, but I'd find him.

I continued sleeping in the living room. I refused to sleep in our bed.

The doorbell rang a few days later, and I stupidly answered it. There was a group of people in hazmat suits, carrying signs—The Crow Posse. I tried to close the door, but they kept pushing on it and yelling things I didn't understand about Tiers and evaluations. I also heard them calling me a CP and "Crow." Even though there were many of them and one of me, I managed to get the door closed. While they continued to bang against the door and shout nonsense, I called the police.

Weeks went by, and they kept up the harassment. Someone egged my car, and another poured a pool of tar onto our front sidewalk. Tom came over and scraped it off for me, then he scoured the area until it looked more normal. Crow Posses would block my front door, forcing me to go out the back and through the yard to get to my car. Spy Patrol guys would camp out on my curb, outside my therapist's office, and even in the IKEA parking lot. When I tried to talk on the phone, I could hear the beep of the call waiting interrupting us, over and over, but no one would be on the line.

Marie and Jeanine teamed up to fight the Faction, the Crow Posse, the Spy Patrol, and anyone else they threw at us. Thing was, Marie and Jeanine were technically CPs, too. The Spy Patrol started to follow them around, and both of them installed cameras outside their front doors in an attempt to ward off the worst of the vandalism. (Eggs, they could deal with. Spray paint, box cutters, setting fire to the lawn, no.) Maybe we should have started a support group. Maybe there already was one. Marie hired a private investigator. He turned up a lot of information we already had, but nothing on Jeff's whereabouts. These Church people could work for the FBI. They really knew how to hide people.

I became a workaholic. That was the temporary, get-through-this plan. Work all of the time, never be home until I was so exhausted I wouldn't notice Jeff wasn't in the house. IKEA usually had plenty of work for me to do, and when they didn't, I'd spend time walking through their showroom, picking out furniture for imaginary homes I might have some day. Some were tiny and cramped, like a city apartment, some were big and as high-end as IKEA got. My pretend design plans went from subdued to IKEA-outrageous, with flower-power wallpaper and shocking pink wardrobes.

I stopped listening to music.

I lost track of time. Days, weeks, going on months... it

seemed endless. Every day was the same: me without Jeff.

Jeanine offered to take me to the mall. She thought a little shopping might be therapeutic, and while I didn't think anything would help, I agreed to go. I managed to leave my house without the Crow Posse stopping me, only to find Jeanine outside, washing her car.

"What are you doing?" I said.

"They wrote 'Surrender CP' on my windshield in soap. I need to get it off before we can go anywhere."

"At least it's only soap."

I grabbed a rag and helped her.

Jeanine drove us to the Roosevelt Field mall in Garden City. I used to love walking around that town when Jeff and I lived there. There were pineapple images everywhere, pressed into metal plates on the sidewalks, printed on street signs, on posters, everywhere. It was supposed to be a symbol of hospitality. When we got to the mall, I suddenly understood why Marie would get carried away there. They had great stores. Trying on clothes definitely took my mind off of Jeff for a few minutes. I had lost weight since he disappeared, so I actually needed some new clothes.

We decided to get an early dinner. There was a seafood place on the ocean side of the Island where Jeanine liked to go to with Tom. I'd never been there. It was remarkably affordable for what it was. We each ordered lobster bisque and the salmon, and after dessert, no matter how much I argued, Jeanine insisted on paying.

It was dark when we were heading back to Floral Park.

Jeanine had me laughing, and we even turned on her Sirius radio and tuned in to the Beatles station.

Then, there was a problem.

"We're being followed," she said.

"We are?"

She turned on her back-view camera. There was a red pick-up truck trailing closely behind us. One might have guessed it was just an average jerk, but when we changed lanes, the truck did too.

"Yeah. We're being followed. That's our third lane change in the last few minutes."

"Great. Now what?"

"I think we need to get rid of him," she said.

"How?"

"Not sure."

She took the next exit, turned onto a side street, and pulled over. The truck pulled over, too, leaving a car length or two between us. We sat there a moment while Jeanine contemplated her next move. The driver behind us waited. Then Jeanine put the car in reverse, backed up, and pulled around to the driver's side of the truck. He took off.

I started laughing. Jeanine was smiling.

"The Faction can kiss my ass," she said.

I was sitting at my kitchen table one morning, and, although I had no appetite to speak of, I was trying to force down a bagel. I heard people loudly singing a Britney Spears song. I went into the living room, looked out the window, and saw a group of Spy Patrol roaches sitting on my lawn. I opened the front door to shoo them away, but they wouldn't budge. Their caterwauling was getting the attention of the neighbors, who by now were no strangers to the odd assortment of visitors in my yard. I closed the door, closed my eyes, and started to chant under my breath, "Stop it. Stop it. Stop it. Stop it. Stop it...." When they started singing their fourth song with no end in sight, I called the police. Singing Britney Spears songs had to be a violation of something.

Marie called later to share the latest report from the private eye. There wasn't a lot of new information, but he found there were indeed people who had been held by the Church. The official explanation was that they were being "treated." There were several hidden Philomathics locations in the tri-state area, although the investigator couldn't find where any of these places were. Most people he had spoken to escaped without ever knowing where they had been held. Marie told him to keep looking.

"Hold on a second," she said to me. "Someone's at my door."

I wanted to tell her not to answer it, but she had already put down the phone. I heard her open the door and then heard a group of people shout, "Where's your son, Marie?" She slammed the door. When she came back to the phone, she was crying.

"When is this going to end?"

When, indeed.

Marie, Jeanine, and I continued to search the internet for clues. Maybe we could find one of those hidden locations the private eye was trying to uncover. We found nothing. I was even considering camping out on the center's steps to wait for Floyd and beg him to tell me where they were hiding Jeff. Something was terribly wrong if I wanted to see Floyd.

I came home one day to find four of the airline-steward people, two men and two women, sitting on my steps. As I got closer, I realized one of them was Helen.

I started yelling: "Helen! Where's Jeff? Is he home? Did you bring him to me?"

They all had Floyd Face. They stood up. Helen was as robotic as the rest of them.

"Where is he? Tell me!"

They walked down the steps to the walkway.

"Tell me where he is, damn it!"

They turned and continued down the sidewalk.

"Tell me!"

Jeanine came out of her house.

"Melody. What's going on?"

I was pointing down the street.

"Those people from the Church. They were sitting on my steps. With Helen. She knows where Jeff is! She won't tell me!" I was wailing.

Other neighbors were coming out of their houses. The stewards from the Church continued walking without the slightest break in their stride. Jeanine led me inside her house.

I sat at her kitchen table and she put the kettle on to boil.

"They're torturing you for their own amusement," she said.

She handed me a box of tissues and sat down with me.

"I can't take much more of this," I said. "I can't believe

they can just hold Jeff captive. It's been months. What if he's willingly staying away from me?"

"I doubt he's willingly doing anything. Marie said the private eye found a lot of cases where people were held against their will, right? I'm sure that's what's going on."

"But what if it isn't? What if Jeff chose them over me? What if he's with Helen?"

Jeanine smirked. "Seriously. You can't possibly believe that."

The kettle started whistling, and she got up to get it.

"I don't know what to believe," I said. "Every day, I think I'm going to wake up and he'll be there. And then he's not, and I spend another day without him."

She poured two cups of tea and sat down again.

"They can't hold him forever. Sooner or later, he's bound to break free."

"Well, he better hurry. I'm becoming completely unhinged."

"Yes, you are."

Somehow, that made me laugh.

I was practically getting used to people constantly ringing my bell, pounding on my door, vandalizing my house, spying on me, calling my phone every few minutes. But then, one day ... nothing. No Crow Posse. No Faction. No Spy Patrol. No Blue Meanies. I could walk out my door, drive to work, go to the gym, talk on the phone. They abruptly started to ignore me.

It was inexplicable, but then I realized: This was worse. I was no longer a threat. They had Jeff, and they were keeping him. Isolation, complete.

Epilogue

Something internal — maybe a dream—woke me from where I was sleeping on the couch. It took a moment for me to get oriented. There was no moonlight, and, it being early morning, no cars were driving by the house. I stared into the dark, Jeff-less room and waited for my eyes to adjust.

It was so quiet.

Without the constant agitation of the Church's goon squads, Jeff's absence was all too real, all too permanent. Those crazy months were something of a distraction. Now, I had all kinds of time to notice that I was alone.

I didn't go back to sleep, I don't think. I was horizontal and motionless, but not escaping into dreams. As the room lightened, I heard birds chirping. One in particular was awfully loud, cutting through the silence in my life, mocking me.

Taking my cue from the birds, I got up off the couch

and went to make coffee. I had a full day planned: running with Laura, working at IKEA, a lunch break with Jeanine, then dinner with Marie and Frank after work. I was trying to get used to my new reality. It wasn't working.

Laura arrived a couple of hours later.

"Ready?" she said.

She never forced conversation, which I appreciated. Others would try to engage me, ask about work, talk about the weather, mention how much they liked my clothes, talk about themselves. Most people eventually gave up; it wasn't fun having a one-sided conversation.

We were having a brutal July. Laura and I were armed with plenty of water and sunscreen, but even so, when we got to the park, we stopped by the pond to splash water on our faces. We kept our run short, went only once around the pond, then headed back to our respective homes to get ready for work. It still seemed strange to me that we weren't going to the same office, but then, a lot of things were strange now.

I got in my car and turned on NPR to have some background noise; although, I found their radio voices to be kind of depressing. I didn't want to be soothed. On the other hand, the alternative, the shock jocks on the other stations, were worse. I didn't want to be yelled at, either.

I was heading to Hicksville on the highway and switched to the fast lane. Somehow, I had turned into a more confident driver since last March. People stopped beeping at me to move over, to go faster, to make the turn. While there were still a lot of assholes on the road, at least I was no longer one of them. I saw the blue and yellow IKEA building appear over the hill, and I actually smiled.

Work: My solace.

Except for a day of rain here or there, the heat just wouldn't let up. By late August, a month where everything in North America was in flames, we were being told to conserve water. One Saturday morning, when IKEA didn't have work for me, I took a long run in the park. I had some thinking to do. James Santini had called to offer me a position as a Senior Interior Designer in Malmö, Sweden. While I would never have contemplated such a move before, with Jeff gone, I was now considering it. There were a whole host of reasons to accept this and very few to keep me in Long Island anymore. A huge change would be good for me. It was a big decision, however—I mean, Malmö?— so I went running in the August heat.

I ran around the pond, then I circled the park the other way and back again. It was blistering, but I just kept running. When I couldn't run anymore, I started home.

I splashed some of the water I was carrying onto my face, then drank some. I never ran with my sunglasses on, but now that I was walking, I wished I had them. A dog started barking at me through its owners' screen door, and the large tuxedo cat next door to him sat lazily on his porch, watching me walk past. As I approached the Giordanis' house, I stopped abruptly. Someone was sitting on my steps. Oh, Jesus, now what? I turned around, ready to run the other way, but then I heard someone call my name.

Was that Floyd?

I walked closer.

It was Jeff.

"Uh... Uh..." That was my big greeting to him. I staggered towards him.

He laughed.

Laughed.

"But... what... where.... How...?"

He stood up, and I ran into his arms, sobbing like a child. When we came up for air, he was smiling. Like a normal person.

"But.... How... What..." I couldn't believe he was in front of me. He was wearing a Philomathics t-shirt and khaki shorts that I didn't recognize, and he was seared with sunburn.

"Look," he said. "Can we go inside? I'm burning up."

I handed him my water bottle, and he gulped down what was left. I was so excited my hands were shaking as I turned the key in the lock. While he stood in front of the air conditioner, I went into the kitchen. I ran a dish towel under the faucet, and I was going to fill a glass with water, then realized we still had a big bottle of Gatorade in the fridge. He drank like he had never experienced liquid before and then pressed the towel on his burned neck and face.

I tried to make light of things, even though I was still sniffling. I said, pseudo-casually, "So... what brings you here?"

It was so good to hear him laugh.

"I escaped," he said. We sat down in the window. I put my hand on his thigh. He was hot from the sun, but he was real, all right. "I was in really bad shape. I was unable to respond to much and getting worse every day. I didn't even know how much time was passing. All I wanted to do was lie down, but they kept forcing me to go to assessments and these weird special treatments for depressed people."

"Treatments?"

He looked at me, then frowned and shook his head.

"Like... they duct-taped my mouth and then commanded me to answer questions. If I didn't respond, they'd slap me and tell me I was failing the Pathway. After about an hour of me futilely screaming through the duct tape, they would tell me I did well. Crazy shit like that. Anyway, on one of my more lucid days, I was going through my things, looking for my razor, and I found this bottle of meds I'd been avoiding..."

He reached into his pocket and took out the vial of antidepressants.

"...and I thought, what did I have to lose? So, I took one."

He put the vial back in his pocket.

"I started to feel a little more normal, more like myself, so I kept taking them."

"And... They just let you go?"

"Ha. No. When I told them that I wanted to go home, they said I needed to stay, that it was for my own good. They physically stopped me from leaving, said I just *thought* I wanted to go. They had the doors locked and everything. And every time I told them I wanted to see you, they said I couldn't because you were a CP."

"How did you get out?" I was practically whispering. My voice was shot from crying.

"I kept asking to leave. I kept demanding to see you. I was making too much noise. I was upsetting people's quest for the Pathway, or some such nonsense. This morning, I was heading to the cafeteria to buy breakfast, and I saw the upper-Tier people who ran the place. I told them I no longer cared about the stupid Pathway, I just wanted out. That finally did it. They unlocked the doors and basically threw me out without any of my things. All I had was what was in my pockets, so just my wallet and my meds. I looked around, and there was nothing, just grass and trees and some dirt paths. No stores. No houses. No streets. I had no idea where I was."

He paused to guzzle the rest of the Gatorade. The towel I had given him was now warm, and he put it on the bench beside him.

"I walked down one of the trails until I eventually found a house. It was this great big absurd house that could have lodged several families. I rang the bell. It took a while, but someone finally answered the door. I asked to use his phone. He saw the logo on my t-shirt and asked me if I was from the Philomathics Center, and I said yes. He asked me if I wanted to call the police, but I said no, I just wanted to go home. I didn't have my phone, and I stupidly couldn't remember anyone's number. The guy wouldn't let me in the house, but he did call a car service for me. It was a long trip, but I got here. I didn't have my keys, so I waited on the steps."

I was trying to talk, but nothing was coming out. It was like I was in one of those dreams, where you try to move, but you can't, you try to run, but you can't, you try to scream, but you can't. He spoke again.

"I realized two very important things."

I wiped my eyes with my hand. He smiled, his Real-Jeff, green-eyed smile.

"One is, I love you. Which, I know, you thought maybe I'd forgotten."

I started crying again. I found part of my voice, and croaked out, "And the other?"

"I fucking hate Philomathics." And he laughed.

This was the best news ever.

"Do you know," he said, "Floyd told me I couldn't listen to music? Now what kind of crazy horseshit is that?"

It was crazy, all right, like all of the other craziness the Philomathists had imposed on us.

"The thing is, they got me pretty well indoctrinated." He was exhibiting Floyd Face, but then he shook his head and rubbed his eyes. "I feel guilty for leaving. I feel like I failed. I'm anxious because I left the Pathway, like I don't know what to do with myself now. How am I going to purge myself from all this crap that's in my head?"

"We'll both have to work on that," I said.

Outside the window, I thought I saw a man in a plaid jacket hiding in the Giordanis' new hedges. I must have been wrong, though; no one was there when I looked again.

About Atmosphere Press

Atmosphere Press is an independent, full-service publisher for excellent books in all genres and for all audiences. Learn more about what we do at atmospherepress.com.

We encourage you to check out some of Atmosphere's latest releases, which are available at Amazon.com and via order from your local bookstore:

This Side of Babylon, a novel by James Stoia
Within the Gray, a novel by Jenna Ashlyn
Where No Man Pursueth, a novel by Micheal E. Jimerson
Here's Waldo, a novel by Nick Olson
Tales of Little Egypt, a historical novel by James Gilbert
For a Better Life, a novel by Julia Reid Galosy
The Hidden Life, a novel by Robert Castle
Big Beasts, a novel by Patrick Scott
Alvarado, a novel by John W. Horton III
Nothing to Get Nostalgic About, a novel by Eddie Brophy
GROW: A Jack and Lake Creek Book, a novel by Chris S
    McGee
Home is Not This Body, a novel by Karahn Washington
Whose Mary Kate, a novel by Jane Leclere Doyle
Stuck and Drunk in Shadyside, a novel by M. Byerly
These Things Happen, a novel by Chris Caldwell
The Glorious Between, a novel by Doug Reid
Sink or Swim, Brooklyn, a novel by Ron Kemper

About the Author

Connecticut born, Robin D'Amato moved to New York City to attend New York University, fell in love with the City, and never left. She has worked in the publishing industry as a pre-press specialist since 1984, when she was introduced to the Macintosh computer. She spent several decades pursuing dance and choreography, but now just dances recreationally. She lives in Manhattan's East Village with her 2,000-LP music room and her two cats.

CPSIA information can be obtained
at www.ICGtesting.com
Printed in the USA
LVHW030418190221
679469LV00008B/475